Diamonds and Dust

Robin Gibson

Other books by Robin Gibson:

The Ruination of Dan Becker

Ma Calhoun's Boys

Riders of Black Dawn

Tucker's Treasure

The Sheriff of Whiskey City

The Bandits of Whiskey City

The Legend of Whiskey City

The Doctor of Whiskey City

The Duchess of Whiskey City

The Warriors of Whiskey City

All rights reserved.
ISBN: 10: 0692343334
ISBN-13: 978-0692343333

DEDICATION

To Kara Jolene Gibson

CHAPTER ONE

On this, the first day of June, a wicked sun blazed across the land. Shimmering heat waves danced across the horizon, distorting the view of the mountains in the far off distance. Spring had been unnaturally warm and as summer arrived, the grass fried to a crisp brown as the ground baked. This left the residents of Cordova praying for rain.

A lone man sat astride a gray horse watching the town from atop a nearby ridge. He didn't care about the grass, or the heat. He sat unmoving with both hands on the saddle horn. Two Smith and Wesson .44 revolvers hung from holsters on his lean hips. Rollie Dukes was a careful man and he believed that if he needed a gun, it'd be best to have two. Along with the two pistols, a Henry rifle rode in the boot hanging from his saddle and rolled up in his bedroll rested a double barreled shotgun. He was a man used to trouble, and ready for it.

Rollie Dukes was on a mission; a mission to find a man.

Would Claude Baines be here? That was the question. Several times, Rollie had thought he might have caught up with Baines only to learn that the man had moved on. Somehow it felt different this time. Baines was here. Rollie could feel it.

Be nice to finally get to it and put the whole mess behind him.

An uncomfortable feeling crept over Rollie. He always felt a little chill when he thought of that night so many years ago. For perhaps the thousandth time, Rollie wished he had ridden around that town.

Rollie smoked and watched the town, feeling a reluctance to ride down. Occasionally, he would raise his head, looking to the

5

mountains looming in the distance. Rollie didn't care about the mountains, except as a possible place of refuge. A place to hide if the need arose.

Rollie had a feeling it would. Claude Baines was a hard man.

Deliberately, he took out the makings and rolled another smoke. The gray shook his head impatiently, as Rollie sat motionless, studying the town. As he smoked, the sun climbed higher in the sky, and the temperature soared. Today would be boiling hot, well over a hundred.

Crushing out the cigarette on the saddle horn, Rollie touched a spur to the gray. The horse stepped out smartly, picking his way daintily down the rock strewn slope. A dog ran out, barking its challenge, but the gray horse paid him no attention. Undaunted, horse and rider continued an even pace toward town. Satisfied with his warning, the dog retreated back to his shady spot watching the stranger continue on his way.

Rollie saw a quick flash of a face in a window, then the shutter was pulled shut. Rollie frowned, it was mighty hot to have the shutters closed. Now, shutters were a handy thing to have during an Indian attack, but they sure blocked out any breeze. On a day like today, without a breeze, the inside of that house would soon be like an oven.

Shaking his head in wonder, Rollie turned his horse toward the stable. Working at his anvil, in front of the livery, the blacksmith paused, hammer in hand to watch the stranger. Squinting against the glare of the early morning's sun, the smith swore, dropping the hammer. He recognized the type.

It wasn't just the two guns which gave Rollie away; it was his quiet, constant vigilance. "Another one, that's all we need," the blacksmith muttered, wiping the sweat from his face. He stood hands on hips and offered no greeting.

"Morning," Rollie said quietly and got a cold stare in return. "How much to stable my horse for a few days?" Rollie's eyes took in the fact that the smith wore a revolver, and had a rifle leaning close by. Quite a lot of hardware to be packing; it made Rollie wonder.

"You'll be wanting oats for him?" the blacksmith asked knowingly, and Rollie nodded. "That'll be six bits a day. Cheaper most other places, but oats is hard to come by in these parts."

Rollie leaned back in the saddle, he could have gotten a friendlier sounding greeting from a rattlesnake. The blacksmith's tone made his attitude clear. He didn't care for Rollie's type and wasn't crazy about keeping his horse.

Rollie stepped down from the gray, leaving the reins trailing in the dust. Unflinchingly, he met the cool stare of the blacksmith. From his pocket, Rollie took the required amount of change and passed it to the burly blacksmith.

The smith grudgingly took the money, jerking his head towards the barn. "You can put him in the back stall. There's water and hay by the back door. I'll bring around the oats."

"Obliged," Rollie grunted, wondering what in blazes was going on here. The smith was packing enough hardware to fight a small war, and was surly as a cornered wolf. Folks were boarded up like they were expecting the devil himself to come riding down the street.

Shaking his head a little, Rollie led the gray into the stall, stripping off the saddle. Whatever was going on here, the smith was sure enough expecting trouble. Judging from what he saw with the window, the smith wasn't the only one. There was trouble here.

As he rubbed the gray, Rollie wondered if Claude Baines could be involved in the trouble. Baines was a braggart and bully, but he was also a hard, mean man. The kind of man who sought out trouble. Always ready to take the advantage.

A bucket of water hung at the front of the stall, but the water was warm and stale. As he pondered the strange doings in this place, Rollie emptied the stale water, refilling it with fresh water from the pump.

"I like a man that takes care of his horse," the smith said, bringing a small bucket of oats.

Rollie smiled, scratching the horse between the ears. "He's brought me a far piece."

"Good animal," the smith said, dumping the oats in a small trough.

"He is that," Rollie agreed. "Name's Dukes, Rollie Dukes."

7

The smith nodded, thinking he had heard the name before. "Hartshorn," he grunted extending his hand.

Rollie took his hand, shaking it firmly. "Where's the best place in town to eat?" he asked, untying his bedroll.

"Place down the street called the Chuckwagon," was the cool answer.

"Good place?"

"Good enough."

Seeing that he wasn't going to get much out of the smith, Rollie tucked the bedroll under his arm and ambled up the street toward the café. Right now all he wanted was a meal and a hot bath. Maybe a drink and a few hours sleep, then he would deal with Claude Baines.

Walking slowly, Rollie noticed a tall, whip-thin man leaning against the awning post out in front of the saloon. As Rollie watched out of the corner of his eye, the man pushed away from the post, stepping into the street. Slowly, insolently, he strode to the center of the street, stopping directly in front of Rollie's path. Hooking his thumbs in his gun belt, he cocked his head sideways and spat in the street.

"Just where do you think you are going?" he snarled.

Rollie stopped, smiling at the man. "If it is any of your business, I'm heading up to the café then over to the hotel," Rollie replied, taking a better grip on his bedroll.

The man shook his head, showing a leering smile. He poked a finger at Rollie. "Take a piece of good advice, friend. Crawl back on that gray hoss and go back to where you come from. Ain't nothing but grief for you here."

Now, Rollie Dukes wasn't a man known for his gentle ways, nor his easy going temperament. Fact was, times like this, he could be downright impatient. Today he was tired and hungry, in no mood for any nonsense. Not bothering to waste words, Rollie whipped up the bedroll, smacking the man across the head with it. The shotgun rolled inside of the bedroll thumped the man across the jaw with the sound of an ax chopping green wood. A slight groan whimpered out of the man as he crumpled to the ground.

Stepping over the fallen man, Rollie tipped the bedroll over his shoulder and calmly continued his way up the street. A rather large woman, with graying hair and a wide smile met him at the door of the Chuckwagen. She held the door open for him, beaming from ear to ear.

"Come right on in, mister. I'll fetch you some coffee. I reckon you'll be wanting a bite to eat."

"Sure," Rollie said, heading for a table in the back. "Whatever you got."

"Eggs! For you, we got eggs!" she exclaimed. "Mind you, we don't serve eggs to just anybody. But today, we sure enough got 'em for you."

Rollie grunted a thank you as he dropped into his chair. Out of habit, he took a quick survey of the room. All of the tables stood empty, which wasn't surprising at this time of morning. Most folks would already be out working.

The waitress brought him his coffee, setting the steaming cup on the table in front of him. "Food'll be ready in just a minute. My husband is cooking it up. He does all the cooking, which by the way is why we call it the Chuckwagen. He used to cook on the trail drives."

Rollie pointed up at the sign. "You know that's spelled...?"

The woman rolled her eyes and snorted. "Oh yeah, I know." She shook her head. "My fool husband cain't spell and cain't admit when he's wrong neither."

Rollie nodded, but he wasn't really listening. Fact was, her steady drone of chatter was making him drowsy. He'd been riding most of the night, something he really didn't enjoy. But when he had heard that Baines was in Cordova, he had pushed hard. Baines had already slipped away from him twice, and Rollie wasn't about to let it happen again.

"Say, what you got in that bedroll? An oak club?" Rollie glanced up as the woman poked a finger at him. "Maybe, you're putting too much starch in your underwear?" she added snorting.

Rollie laughed a little. He was starting to like this woman. "No. I gotta shotgun rolled up in there."

She nodded, "That would do it I reckon. Land sakes, you sure laid into Carney. It done my heart good to see it, too. Lord knows, he's had it coming."

"Who had it coming?" a huge, hairy man carrying a platter of food asked.

9

"Carney," the woman said, then waved a hand in Rollie's direction. "He stretched ol' Carney out cold in the street. Smacked him upside the head with a shotgun."

A smile broke across the big man's red face. "No foolin?" he asked, glancing at Rollie who nodded.

"I just told you he did!" the woman snapped, stamping her foot. "Now give the poor man his food, before he starves to death."

The cook shot his wife a dark scowl, as he slapped the platter of food on the table. He waited until she turned her back, then shook his fist at her. "You want some more coffee?" she asked, turning back with the coffee pot in hand.

Watching the pair, Rollie had to smile. He had actually heard the old cook's shoulder pop, as his wife spun back around. The way he jerked his fist out of the air, it was a wonder his whole arm didn't come unhinged. Winking at Rollie, the cook covered his movements by hitching the plate of food closer to Rollie. "Food's on the house, just for decking Carney."

"Thanks," Rollie grunted, glancing down at the plate of food. The plate held three eggs, two thick slices of bread and a large slab of beef steak.

"Don't suppose you kilt him?" the cook asked, and Rollie shook his head. "Shoot, too much to hope for, I reckon," the old cook said with real sadness in his voice.

"That's a hard thing to say," Rollie commented.

"Not if you know Carney. Killings too good for him if you ask me," she snapped, lowering her head a mite as she glared at him.

It reminded Rollie of a bull about to charge, and he surely didn't want to be the target of that charge. "Sure, sure," he said hurriedly. "I'm sure he had it coming."

"Sure did," the cook agreed, then sighed, shaking his head. "I've been thinking of doing that myself. Swatting Carney upside the head, I mean," the big cook said in a booming voice, as his wife snorted. "I have been! Just been waiting for the devil to give me a real good excuse."

For his part, Rollie had little doubt but what the old cook could do it. Though middle-aged, the cook was a bull-strong man, built like a mud brick, with heavy muscles on his shoulders. He had a wide florid face, with a meaty nose that looked to have been broken several times.

"This Carney, he make a practice of jumping strangers?" Rollie asked, as he spread butter across the bread.

"He makes a practice of jumping anyone who walks down the street," the cook replied. "It's his job, but I reckon he enjoys it."

"He works for Charles W. Tinsworth," the woman supplied, her tone saying what she felt about Tinsworth.

"Does a feller by the name of Claude Baines work for Tinsworth? " Rollie asked, pausing from his food just long enough to ask the question.

The cook's bushy eyebrows shot up. "No," he said slowly. "Baines works for Hank Bickerstaff. Do you know Claude, Mister ah...?"

"Dukes. Rollie Dukes," Rollie supplied, laying down his fork to take the big man's hand.

"Ivan Moser. That mean old bag there is my wife Ethel."

"You best watch your step old man or you'll find yourself sleeping in the outhouse," Ethel warned, shooting the old cook a look that woulda soured whiskey.

"Do you know where I can find Baines?" Rollie asked, continuing his assault on the plate of food.

"I imagine he'll be out at Bickerstaff's ranch. The whole crew usually comes into town on Saturday night," Ethel said, taking the plate as Rollie pushed it away.

While Ethel gathered the silverware and took them into the kitchen to be washed, Ivan lumbered over to the counter. He took a cup from the shelf, and the coffee pot from the small stove. "You and Claude friends?" he asked, filling Rollie's cup. He looked critically at his own cup, wiping a spot with the tail of his shirt before filling it.

Rollie smiled at him over the top of his cup. "Friends? No. Fact is, I mean to kill him," Rollie stated in a smug manner.

If he expected the big cook to be shocked, Rollie was in for a big disappointment. The cook merely sipped his coffee a thoughtful expression wrinkling his brow. "He do something to you?"

Rollie didn't answer. He was warming up to the old cook, but didn't want to get into his reason right now. Even though Rollie had never met Moser before, he knew the type. Those old trail cooks were a breed of their own. They had to ride herd on a bunch of rowdy young cowhands and Moser looked fit for the job. Just under six feet tall, he must have weighed all of two hundred fifty pounds. Not much of it was fat either. He barely showed his age, though his red curly hair was beginning to turn gray.

Moser frowned seeing that he wasn't going to get much out of this man. The cook sighed, knowing it wouldn't be any good to push. "You best be careful, son, Bickerstaff has a bunkhouse crammed full of gun hands," Ivan told him. "They ain't gonna look kindly on that kind of talk."

That took Rollie somewhat by surprise. This is a small quiet looking town; he hadn't expected to run into the middle of a range war here. "Seems to be a lot of fighters around here," he commented.

A worried frown crossed Ivan's face. "Been a lot of trouble around here lately," he explained. "There's gonna be more too. Might be best if you just crawled on your horse and showed this place your tail feathers."

It sounded like good advice, but Rollie was a stubborn man. He came here for Claude Baines and he was going to get him. "I'd like to hear all about it, but right now I need some sleep," Rollie said, finishing his coffee and sliding the cup across the table.

When Rollie reached in his pocket, Ivan shook his head. "No need for that. Like I said before, it's on the house." Moser shook his head and grinned ruefully, "I wish I coulda seen you stretch out Carney, though." Moser extended his hand. "You come back any time."

Rollie took the rough hand the cook offered, then started for the door. The sound of Moser's voice stopped him. "Before you do anything, come talk to me."

With a shrug, Rollie opened the door. He wasn't sure another talk with the old cook would accomplish much. Rollie wasn't interested in the problems of the town, he wanted to finish his job and get along.

Rollie stepped out of the café, pausing to roll a smoke. He looked up the street. The town looked quiet enough.

12

Either Carney had woke up or someone had helped him, because he was gone from the street. Not that it mattered to Rollie; all he cared about was getting into a soft bed at the hotel.

Rollie was mounting the boardwalk in front of the hotel when a tall man in a tailored suit stopped him. "I'm Charles W. Tinsworth."

The man had a self-important attitude which got right under Rollie's skin. Unimpressed, Rollie leaned against the awning and took out the makings for a smoke.

Tinsworth forced a smile and ran a hand over his slicked down hair. "You would be Rollie Dukes?"

"Word travels fast in this town," Rollie replied, impatient with the delay.

"Yes, quite so. I have a proposition for you Mister Dukes. How would you like to go to work for me?"

The man's arrogance angered Rollie and if Carney was a sample of what he hired, Rollie wanted no part of it. "I don't need a job."

"I'm willing to offer top dollar, maybe a little better for a man of your obvious caliber," Tinsworth said, grabbing Rollie by the arm.

"I don't know you, Tinsworth, but I heard you was a low down dog." Tinsworth's face pinched in anger and his grip tightened on Rollie's arm. "Take your hand off me," Rollie said, looking pointedly at Tinsworth's hand on his arm. "I won't ask you twice."

Tinsworth turned white with anger and for a wild instant he thought about using the derringer he carried up his sleeve. It was on a spring-loaded clip and Tinsworth knew how fast he could get it out. But Carney was supposed to be fast and he hadn't even slowed this man down.

Tinsworth relaxed and let his hand fall from Rollie's shoulder. "That's dangerous talk friend," Tinsworth hissed through clenched teeth.

"Yeah? You just do something about it," Rollie said softly, daring the big man.

But Tinsworth had gotten control of his temper, he even managed a tight, little smile. "One of these days I might just do that," he replied, chomping on his cigar. He ran his hand through his hair. "Take some good advice and keep on riding. You'll find nothing but trouble here."

Turning his back on the big dude, Rollie stepped through the door into the hotel. An attractive woman stood behind the counter, with a newspaper in front of her. Tall and queenly looking, her long dark hair accentuated her cream colored skin.

"Can I help you?" she asked, with elaborate politeness.

"I need a room and a bath," Rollie said, leaning his bedroll against the counter.

She studied Rollie for a long instant before replying. "I don't want any trouble here," she warned.

"No need to worry about that. I'm a peace loving man myself," Rollie promised, giving her a wide grin.

From her pinched expression, Rollie got the impression she didn't believe him. "If you're not, I'll send you packing," she replied coolly.

Rollie laughed, liking her spunk. "You look kinda young to be running a place like this."

"My age is none of your concern," she snapped, sliding the register across the scarred counter top. "Sign here, or make your mark," she instructed. Rollie scribbled his name and pushed the book back. She glanced at the register, then held out a key. "Here's your key, Mister Dukes. Your room is the second door on the left at the top of the stairs. The bath house is through there," she said, indicating a hallway.

While Rollie had his bath and nap, he was being talked about by Ivan Moser and John Hartshorn, the blacksmith. Moser was pacing, rubbing his hands together. "He could be just the man for the job."

The smith frowned, worry written on his broad face. "I don't know. He looks like trouble to me," he said, as he pumped the bellows of his forge.

"Of course he's trouble, but not for us. I think he can be trusted," Moser argued, waving away Hartshorn's concerns. "He is a hard man, but it'll take a hard man for the job. We can't wait long, or we'll have another dead body on our hands," Ivan warned.

John critically inspected his metal before answering. "Aye, you're right about that. We've got to stop the killing, but I'm afraid hiring Dukes will only lead to more killing," John replied gloomily.

Ivan Moser nodded emphatically. "That's the way I figure it. I figure either Dukes will catch the killer or get himself killed trying.

At best we get our problem solved; the worst thing that can happen is we end up right where we started."

Moser looked both ways lowering his head a mite. "I got an idea," he whispered. "An idea of how we might be able to use this feller Dukes." Moser chuckled rubbing his hands together. "Yes sir, Dukes might come in right handy."

"With Jim gone is this still gonna work?" Hartshorn wondered.

"I dunno," Moser replied, pacing again. "If we could get this feller Dukes to throw in with us, it still might be okay," he decided.

"We have to talk him into it."

Moser smiled a crooked grin. "Leave that to me. I got myself a notion about that." Moser even giggled a little taking his friend by surprise. "Yes sir, I got an idea. I'll sign him up alright."

Enjoying the warm water, Rollie Dukes leaned back in the tub and lit a cigar. Relaxing in pure comfort, he was thinking of the past. Of a dark night so long ago. The flash of gunfire, and a man dying. He had no idea the town was planning to make him a hero, or get him killed.

CHAPTER TWO

Noon came and went before Rollie woke. By midafternoon, the heat was hammering through the window, making sleep impossible. Yawning, Rollie stretched in the bed, relishing the soft feel of the mattress. He enjoyed the feeling for a moment, then with a sigh blowing past his lips; he sat up, swinging his feet over the edge of the bed. Still sluggish from his sleep, Rollie stumbled across the room to the dresser and poured water from the pitcher into the wash basin. After splashing the cool water on his face, Rollie felt better.

Slipping on a fresh shirt, Rollie checked the loads in both his pistols. He slung the gun belts around his waist, grabbed his hat, and headed to the door. Time to deal with Baines.

Sarah Eckles stood behind the counter folding sheets that looked white and crisp as a new snow bank. She looked up from her work as he pounded down the stairs. "Enjoy your nap?" she asked with a smile.

"I suppose," Rollie replied, hesitating before handing her the key. With the smile on her face, she looked pretty enough to melt a frozen pond. Rollie scuffed his boot on the floor. He desperately wanted to say something, but nothing was coming to mind. "Here," he said, holding out the key. "I'll be back later."

Sarah hung the key back on the board as she watched him leave. She wondered about Rollie Dukes; she couldn't quite put him in any category. She saw the exchange of words he had with Tinsworth and deduced that their meeting had not been a friendly one.

Dukes impressed her with his quiet confidence; he appeared to be in complete control of himself and his surroundings. Though only medium height, his shoulders balanced broad over a rider's lean waist. His blue eyes, strikingly clear, accented the deep tan of his face.

Sarah stamped her foot, angry with herself. She recognized Rollie Dukes for what he was. Young as she was, Sarah had a good reason to know the type. Such a man could come to only one end. Dismissing Rollie from her mind, Sarah returned to her laundry. Still, she couldn't keep from looking up and watching him step off the boardwalk and into the street.

Rollie left the hotel and headed back to the cafe. What Moser had said made sense, it wouldn't be wise to move until he knew just what he was getting into. What he needed to know, was how many men Bickerstaff had, when they would be gone, and where they would go. Rollie knew that crews were fiercely loyal to one another. Rollie had no desire to tangle with a crew of upset cowhands and if Bickerstaff was hiring gun hands, that might take some thinking. Course Baines was a new man, they might not be so willing to lay their lives on the line.

Ivan saw Rollie coming and had the coffee already poured. "Come on in, boy," he boomed, handing Rollie a cup. "I had a notion you'd be back today."

"How many men does Bickerstaff have?" Rollie asked, sliding into a chair.

"Ten to twelve, all of them fighters, too." Moser frowned, and added, "Those who weren't fighters, they done moved on."

"His place pretty spread out?" Rollie wanted to know.

"Some. He's got a couple of line shacks, but I doubt if Baines would be at one of them. Hank usually keeps the new men close to home." Ivan sipped his coffee and studied the quiet man across from him. Although knowing it would be a waste of time, Ivan tried to talk the man out of going. "I don't think it would be a good idea for you to go out there. Matter of fact, you'd best forget the whole idea."

"I can't do that. I've got a score to settle with him." Rollie sloshed the bitter coffee in the cup and decided not to tell Moser the whole story. Still he had to say something. Wouldn't do to get the big cook wondering why he was really here. "Baines ambushed me out in the Mohave. Shot me out of the saddle and took my horse." Rollie was surprised how easily the lie rolled off his tongue.

Rollie didn't elaborate; he didn't have to. Moser would fill in the rest on his own. Rollie knew the cook would probably come up with a better story than Rollie could hope to spin. He blew on his coffee and watched Moser run it through his mind.

Finally the cook nodded. "I'm not saying that I blame you for wanting to check him into boot hill, I'm just warning you to go easy. Folks are on edge. You go round talking of killing you're liable to get your neck stretched." Moser shook his head, a look of sadness riding his face. "I swear, I never saw the like. People are flat out scared."

"What's going on?" Rollie asked.

"Folks been dying left and right, and unless you consider a bullet in the back peaceful, they ain't exactly been going in their sleep."

"Range war?" Rollie asked absently. He wasn't really concerned about the town and its problems, but Ivan felt like talking.

"I don't know," Ivan said turning the coffee cup in his hands. "Could be, though. First one killed was a rancher named Killigan. He owned the biggest spread. He and his brother were the first ones to settle in this country."

"Brother dead too?" Rollie asked, testing the coffee. It was hot and black as midnight.

"Naw. Old Mort's got a claim back in the hills." The old cook hitched his chair a little closer. "There's a rumor running round," Ivan paused and glanced about. Leaning forward he continued in a hushed tone. "Folks around these parts figure the old coot's finally struck the mother lode."

Ivan stared at Rollie intently, waiting for a reaction. Rollie wasn't interested in stories of gold mines. He'd heard a thousand such stories and none of them ever panned out. But the murders were different. They sparked the curiosity in him. "Who else was killed?"

"A homesteader named Brown was shot in the back. There were two others, a hand of Bickerstaff's and a drifter. Then a couple of days back, our sheriff was killed."

Rollie gave a low whistle. Ivan was right, this was not the time to be talking of killing. Rollie had seen a few little places like this one when the folks got riled up. A sight to behold! Mass lynchings of whoever the town thought was deserving were not uncommon. "That's alot of killing."

"You sure ain't woofin'" Moser said sounding glum as a fog bank. "Folks are scared. You see why I said you might want to go easy on the talk about killing Claude Baines."

"You already said that, but you're right. Maybe I should ride on, but I've never been the type to let things be," Rollie said determinedly.

"That's what I figured, which brings me to my point." Moser tasted his coffee before continuing. He set his cup on the table, turning it on the table cloth. "How'd you like to be our new sheriff?"

Rollie wouldn't have been more surprised if Moser had leaned across the table and slapped him. "But you don't even know me," Rollie protested. "For all you know I could be an outlaw myself."

"That's right. But right now we don't much care. This town is scared, Mister, and we need somebody now. Somebody with gumption. I reckon that's you."

Rollie shook his head slowly. The last thing he wanted was to be tied to a job like this. It would take endless hours of investigation to track down the killer or killers as the case might be.

"Look, we might not know much about you, but how much do we need to know?" Moser argued. "We know you can handle yourself. We seen that this morning, when you put the dent in Carney's noggin."

"All I want is to find Baines and move on," Rollie maintained, but without much conviction. To tell the truth, he felt a spark of interest growing. Listening to Moser his mind had been going over the string of killings, and he had a million questions.

Sensing Rollie's hesitancy, Moser pushed on. "You could arrest Baines. Sure haul his sorry carcass in here and if he is guilty, we'll string him up. Be all nice and legal like," Moser promised. "Now, we wouldn't expect you to stay on permanent. Just help us keep the lid on till the killer is found."

Moser rubbed his hands together, a crafty smile sneaking onto his face. "Course if you liked it here, and was of a mind to stay?" Moser scooted his chair closer, leaning halfway across the table. "A man could do well for himself here."

"Oh yeah?" Rollie grunted more to hold up his end of the conversation than for any interest in the answer.

Moser glanced both ways, making sure they were alone. "Now, this may look like a little place, but we got a lot going on here. This place is growing. Gonna be something one day soon, I reckon." Taking another quick peek around, Moser lowered his voice another notch. "Word is the railroad will be coming right through here," he said tapping the table with his massive fingers.

Rollie frowned. "Take a few years for it to get here."

Moser beamed, clapping Rollie on the back. "Dang, boy, I knew you were smart." Moser took a quick gulp of his coffee, wiping his mouth with a quick swipe of the back of his hand. "You're right about that, but we gotta start getting ready. Don't wanna get caught with our backsides hangin out. First thing, me and Hartshorn are thinking of starting a freight company. Bring in supplies from Santa Fe."

"Won't a freight company be useless once the railroad gets here?"

"Sure, maybe," Moser admitted, a trickle of sweat running down his face. "But we can make some good money before then." The cook shrugged, pulling out a handkerchief and mopping his face. "What does it take to start a freight company? Way we figure it; we already have three wagons and three teams of mules. I know where I can buy two more teams dirt cheap. Hartshorn is going to build two more wagons, and we are all set. Now the way I see it, Hartshorn and me will provide the mules and wagons, plus some expense money to get started with. You run the thing and we will split the profits three ways."

"Even splits?"

"Well…," Moser started, then swallowed hard. "Alright, even splits," he decided, bobbing his head up and down.

"I don't know. I can't say I want to drive a freight wagon."

"Oh, sure, wouldn't expect you to," Moser replied quickly. "What we need is somebody to run things, ride along with the wagons, scout for water and keep trouble away. You'd have to dicker for the supplies once you got to Santa Fe."

Moser took another hit from his coffee, dribbling down his chin, "Now there's a new town west of here in the mountains, place called

Flagstaff. They are going to be needing supplies. You'd have to ride over there, set up some contracts to bring in their stuff."

Rollie leaned back in his chair. This sounded like a good opportunity. While he thought, Moser fidgeted in his chair, tracing circles on the table with his coffee cup. "This wouldn't take all your time. You could file on some ground yourself, get a place to run some cattle."

"Then when the railroad comes in, our business will be gone."

"Maybe," Moser admitted, sneaky smile crawling across his face. "Then maybe not. Gonna be lots of little towns that the railroad misses. They'll be needing goods. We got us a warehouse, we unload the stuff here, then freight it out to the other towns."

"Sounds like you have thought this through," Rollie said, rubbing his chin. It did sound good.

"Didn't plan on all this killing, though," Moser said, sourly. "We just gotta stop all this killing." Moser's face clouded. "We got big plans. Hartshorn knows this fella that makes shoes and his wife sews clothes. Now they were all ready to pack up and come here, but now?" Moser spread his hands, his face sour as milk left in the sun. "They might back out."

"What does Hartshorn think about this? Hiring me, I mean."

Moser waved away such concerns with a flick of his hand. "Aw, he worries like an old widder woman, but he'll come around. 'Specially if you can corral this killer. You can handle this fella?"

"Yeah, if I can figure out who he is, I can bring him in."

"Good boy, we have a deal then?"

Rollie drank his coffee and considered the proposal. It held a certain challenge which appealed to him. Still, what did he know about running an investigation? Couldn't be harder than reading trail sign, which Rollie was very good at. Rollie felt a pause; the last thing he wanted was Claude Baines in jail.

"We need some help bad, Rollie. Tinsworth and Bickerstaff have already hired fighters, and some of the smaller ranchers are considering doing likewise. Something don't get done soon, the lid's gonna blow off."

"Let me think about it." Rollie rose from his chair. Shifting his gun, he tossed a quarter on the table and waved off Ivan's attempt to make change. "Keep it. I'll be back later."

After Rollie left, Ivan leaned back in his chair and smiled. He had tickled the quiet stranger's interest. He hoped it would keep Dukes in town. Cordova was headed for trouble and would need a man like Rollie Dukes.

Any man, who could survive, wounded and on foot in the desert, would be canny and tough. And Carney was no pilgrim. That impressive episode in the street told Moser something. Anyone who could dispatch Carney so easily would be a man to be reckoned with. Dukes could have easily killed Carney, but he hadn't. To Moser, that meant Dukes had judgment.

Ethel finished the lunch dishes and sat beside her husband. "Do you think he will take the job?" she asked, drying her red hands on her apron.

Ivan only shrugged his heavy shoulders. Dukes wasn't the type to be pushed into a job he didn't want. For now they could only wait and see. "Better question, you think folks round here will have him?"

Ethel frowned, still rubbing her hands on her apron. "Right now, I think they would make a deal with the devil himself if it would stop all the killing."

After leaving the café, Rollie was at a loss for what to do. No longer sleepy, he still didn't feel like going to the saloon. Feeling cramped by the confines of the town, he decided to take a ride.

Walking down the street toward the stable, Rollie noticed that the street was deserted. Still early in the afternoon, the townspeople should be out doing their business. However, the whole town seemed to be waiting, hiding in fear.

Well maybe not the whole town. Rollie could tell by the ring of the hammer, that the smith was hard at work. The blacksmith pounded at his anvil, as Rollie approached. The rifle still leaned against the anvil. Now Rollie understood why.

"Have you spoken with Moser?" the burly blacksmith asked, laying aside his hammer.

"We talked some. Fact is, he offered me a job," Rollie replied, inspecting the horseshoes. A master of his craft, the smith shaped each shoe exactly the same. Even and perfect. "Actually, he offered me two jobs."

The smith wore a worried frown. "And did you accept, either?"

22

"Not yet. Still thinking it over."

The smith dipped some water from the horse trough and splashed it on his face. "I'm not sure you are the man for the job, but we sure do need somebody."

"You're afraid that I might be just as bad as the man doing the killing?" Rollie asked, as he headed inside the barn to get his horse.

"That's right. After all, you did say you were here to kill a man," the smith bluntly pointed out. "I don't know, but somebody has to deal with this mess."

Rollie smiled at the smith. "What about the other thing?"

Hartshorn sighed. "We don't stop the killing it won't matter." He looked at Rollie seriously. "You stop the killing and I will go along with the other thing. You think you can stop it?"

Rollie shrugged as he tightened the cinch. "One thing that bothers me is a couple of the people who were killed. Moser said a drifter and one of Bickerstaff's cowhands were killed. Makes no sense to kill them."

"What do you mean?" the smith asked, looking more worried all the time. Rollie had the feeling that the same thought had already occurred to the big smith.

"Why bother killing them? Nothing to be gained by it," Rollie asked and the smith groaned, he knew what was coming. "Makes a body wonder if this fella just likes the killing," Rollie commented, climbing aboard the gray. Having spoken his piece, Rollie gathered the reigns and touched a spur to the gray.

The smith watched the stranger ride slowly down the trail. It had bothered him also that those two men had been killed, but he hadn't been willing to accept that there could be someone who killed for the pure enjoyment of it. Shaking his head, the smith took up his hammer and returned to work.

Less than an hour had passed when a shrill scream split the quiet air of Cordova. It came from behind the jail. The storekeeper, Joshua Burke was the first one to the spot.

As he rounded the corner of the jail, Burke ran into a screaming Irma Hartshorn. Irma was the wife of the smith.

"They killed old Ben Riggs!" she screamed.

Ivan and Ethel Moser were right behind Hartshorn. Ethel led the hysterical Irma Hartshorn away, while Ivan and Burke went to see about Riggs.

It wasn't a pretty sight which greeted them behind the jail. Old Ben was lying in a pool of blood. He had been stabbed over a dozen times.

Even though both men knew what they would find, they were shocked by the sheer savagery of the killing. Riggs was the jailor and well over sixty years old. Almost blind, the old jailor presented a threat to know one. Just no reason for anybody to kill him.

"Is it true?" Hartshorn asked, coming up the alley behind them. "Is he dead?"

Moser stepped out of the way so the smith could see the body. Hartshorn swore softly. "Poor ol' Ben. Why would anyone want to hurt him?" John Hartshorn asked in a choked voice. Ivan Moser didn't answer, he just turned away and swore bitterly.

CHAPTER THREE

After Ben Riggs' body had been taken over to the undertaker's, Ivan Moser made the rounds, talking to the townspeople. Moser worked the crowd better than any snake oil salesman. He shook hands and slapped backs, and quietly asked everyone to meet at his café. Ethel handed out cups of steaming coffee as they trickled in. Slowly they shuffled by her, taking their coffee silently. When most of the townsfolk had gathered, Ivan stood and cleared his throat noisily.

"I reckon we all know why we're here," he said, as soon as the noise quieted down. Without waiting for a reply, he continued. "I guess by now you all have heard about poor ol' Ben Riggs."

A murmur circled the room and heads nodded in affirmation. "So, I called you all here to discuss the hiring of Rollie Dukes as our new sheriff."

All of a sudden everybody wanted to talk at once. From the hubbub, Ivan couldn't tell if they were for or against his proposal. Finally, skinny, tired-looking Joshua Burke stood up, and the room slowly quieted again.

"I don't know about that, Ivan. We don't know much about the man, though anyone can see he's nothing but a hard case." Burke looked around the room for support. "No sir, I'd say he isn't our type."

"And I agree," Sarah Eckles stated flatly. She glanced about the room, spreading her hands. "How do we know Dukes would be any better than what we have now?"

Sarah Eckles had lived in Cordova only a year, but in that time she had earned the respect of the whole town. No one knew where she came from. That wasn't a question that was asked. But they knew she came to town with enough money to buy the Empire Hotel. The hotel had done well under her management, and she had shown the town that she was always willing to help those in need. Several times she had helped to nurse the sick. When Bud Swenson's wife had been sick, Sarah rode out to their farm everyday to help Bud take care of the house and see to the two youngsters.

"Sarah is right," Joshua Burke agreed, looking around the crowd for support. "We need a sheriff, but we best hire someone we know."

"You know, you're dang sure right, Joshua," Moser said quickly, slapping a beefy hand down on the counter. "I suppose you'll want to take the job yourself. Whew! That's sure a load off my mind. Snap to and I'll swear you in."

Moser stopped, waiting but Joshua never moved. Turning serious, Moser nodded. "That's what I thought. Look folks, this here ain't gonna be an easy job. It'll take a hard man to do it." The assembly grumbled in protest, but the old cook calmly cut them off. "Joshua, can you afford time away from your store to hunt for this killer?"

Joshua silently hung his head, leaving no doubt to his answer. Sensing the hesitation in the room, Moser pressed on. "Can any of the rest of you? And what would you do if you found him? Are any of you ready to take on this vicious murderer?"

From the total silence which followed Moser's words it was clear that they hadn't considered this. Finally, with a loud sigh, John Hartshorn gave in. "I'm not sure I'm all for this, but we must do something. If Dukes will take the job, maybe we'd best hire him right now."

There might have been some opposition to this, but Marge Ross' booming voice tended to drown out every sound for miles. "Hire Dukes? Well blue blazes, I reckon we'd best do it. Like Moser said, this is going to take a man with hair on his chest and sand in his craw. Now, I've seen this feller Dukes, and I'd say he can handle the job, and he surely is a cut above the rabble that Bickerstaff and Tinsworth have been hiring." Having spoke her piece, Marge eased her heavy frame back into her chair.

In the corner, Ivan Moser smiled. Dukes was as good as hired, now. When Marge Ross spoke her mind, most folks just naturally lost their desire to argue. Moser reckoned that Marge could back up a thunderstorm if she set her mind to it.

Marge lived by herself on a small farm just outside of town. She raised pigs, chickens, and ran a few cows. A large woman, Marge did all the work on the farm herself since the death of her husband several years back. The local joke around town was that he died of fright. Despite the smile which was always plastered across her brown, wrinkled face, she had a steadfast determined quality which showed clear through. Ivan Moser had never seen Marge truly angry and couldn't really imagine it. A small shudder went through him at the thought. All in all, Marge was about as subtle as a battering ram. She spoke her mind plainly, with no two ways about it, and when she spoke, people listened!

It was decided that Moser and John Hartshorn should talk with Rollie at the earliest moment. With a decision made, the crowd broke up quickly, with everyone pondering the outcome of their decision today. Though skeptical, most were hopeful. It eased their minds to think they had done something.

While the people of Cordova held their meeting, Charles W Tinsworth held a council of his own. His men were gathered loosely in the back of the Longhorn Saloon.

Bob Neal, who owned half of the saloon, flittered nervously in the background. Tinsworth was his partner, so Bob could not refuse them their meeting, but he didn't like it. For one he didn't like nor trust Tinsworth, but Bob had owed the bank money, and Tinsworth had taken half interest in the saloon as payment. But more than his dislike for Tinsworth was his fear of Bickerstaff. Neal had known the big rancher for a long time and knew how ruthless he could be. Bickerstaff wouldn't like this. Not at all.

Nervously, Bob set a bottle on the table and scurried to the front to see about his customers. Bob Neal didn't have to hear what was being said, to know it involved the killing and burning of innocent farmers. Neal had seen enough of Tinsworth to know the man was totally lacking in scruples.

"Bickerstaff will try to move in on the Killigan spread today," Lex Taylor said.

27

"Good, let him try," Tinsworth said to the surprise of everyone in the room. "Killigan's crew is still out there. They'll hold Bickerstaff off for a few days."

Blank faces stared at Tinsworth. His men hadn't expected this. It pleased Tinsworth that his men weren't following his train of thought. He always considered himself just a bit smarter than the rest of the world.

White teeth showed as Tinsworth smiled wolfishly. "I've received word that Jim Killigan's niece is going to inherit the ranch and that she's coming here."

"What does that mean?" Carney asked, still sporting a nasty looking bruise.

"It means that the Killigan place is as good as mine," Tinsworth replied, smacking his lips in satisfaction.

Leaning back in his chair, Tinsworth placed his booted feet on the table. "The townspeople are clamoring for a sheriff. It won't be long till they get one, and we must be ready." He paused and looked at each of his men. He was no longer smiling. His eyes gleamed bright and hard, and his jaw was set firmly. "Here's a list of the nesters I want run out," he said tossing a slip of paper across the table.

Sweeping his feet off the table, Tinsworth stood up. Pointing a long finger at his men, he issued his orders. "I want these people run off and I don't care how you do it. Just do it fast and make sure they won't be back."

This brought sadistic smiles to the faces of his men. They were tired of sitting around biding their time. "When they are gone, I want each of you to file a claim on their place. Is that understood?"

Most did, but Taylor still had a question. "What about the Killigan place? It's the biggest, has the best water, and ready for the taking. If we wait around, Bickerstaff will beat us to it."

Tinsworth smirked and clapped Taylor on the back. "You are right about that, but I have that all taken care of,' Tinsworth replied pulling a paper from his vest pocket and tossing it lightly on the table.

"What is that, an I.O.U.?" Carney asked, frowning at the document.

Tinsworth allowed himself another chuckle and took a cigar from his pocket. "It's a loan against the Killigan spread. I'll show it to this niece when she shows up."

Lighting the cigar, Tinsworth returned to this seat. "You men have enough to keep you busy, so you'd better get started."

As his men filed out, Tinsworth drew deeply on his cigar and replaced his feet on the table. Licking his thumb, he rubbed a spot on his shiny black boots.

Things were going so well here! He already owned the bank and half interest in the saloon. He had a small ranch and soon, he was sure he would be the proud owner of the largest ranch in the county. But he wasn't satisfied with that. He wanted the smaller ones, too. Combined they might be as large as the famous Hashknife outfit.

Tinsworth paced the room unable to sit still. Excitement surged through him. Soon he would be one of the wealthiest men in the territory. His opinions would be respected, and he would have power. He might just run for Governor.

It hadn't always been this way for Charles W. Tinsworth, which wasn't even his real name. Like everything else he wanted, Tinsworth took the name. He had come a long way since his boyhood days on the back streets of New Orleans. He began his career by robbing the sailors on the docks, but unlike his friends, young Charles hadn't squandered away his money. From robbery he moved to gambling on the river boats, and the way he played cards there wasn't much difference.

When New Orleans became too hot for him, Charles moved west, proving to be the best move he ever made. The west was wide open and growing, a perfect place for young Charles to operate. Now just a few short years later, he had put together a modest fortune. Here in Cordova, he planned to triple his holdings.

From records he had found in the bank, Tinsworth knew that both Jim and Mort Killigan had been sending money back East to their niece. That bothered Tinsworth. He couldn't figure where the money came from. Jim was no riddle. He owned a large ranch. But Mort? Local opinion of him was unimpressive. Just a harmless old prospector. Where did he get the money? Had he struck it rich?

In his own mind, Tinsworth was sure of it. He was convinced that ol' Mort had found the mother lode. And Tinsworth wanted it.

But how to find the claim? Mort seldom came to town. The niece now, maybe he could use her. By asking a few discreet questions, Tinsworth had found that neither Mort nor Jim had seen their niece in fifteen years. Would Mort trust her enough to tell her where the claim was? Did sending money make you close? Having never been close to anyone in his life, Tinsworth didn't know.

So far things had gone smoothly. Bickerstaff was going to do most of the dirty work and take all the blame. Tinsworth smiled, what a clod. While Bickerstaff floundered around in his blundering way, Tinsworth intended to be moving. He reminded himself to watch Bickerstaff, the man was a rough clod, but he could be dangerous.

Rollie rode slowly into town. He was surprised to find that the smith was not at his anvil. With a shrug, he led the gray inside and began stripping the saddle. As he hung the saddle on the fence, Rollie heard a step behind him. Assuming that it was the smith, Hartshorn, Rollie continued with his task.

"You Rollie Dukes?"

Rollie spun around, his hand falling to the gun on his hip. A fat, dirty man was standing in the huge door. Rollie's reaction brought a smile to his thin lips, revealing broken, yellowed teeth. "Yeah, you would be Dukes alright."

"And you would be Bickerstaff," Rollie acknowledged, eyeing the man with distaste.

Bickerstaff nodded and ran a not-so-clean sleeve across his forehead. As he brought his hand away from his face, the big rancher's attitude changed. "You're a stranger here, so here's a piece of advice; forget why you came here, and leave." His small, black eyes were intense, ashe stood hands on hips. His shirt was filthy and hung out at the bottom. The only thing about him that looked clean and cared for was his gun.

"I came here on business, and I won't leave till it's done," Rollie stated flatly.

A sneer crossed the fat man's face, and sweat trickled across the blue-black stubble on his cheeks. Walking over to the stall, Bickerstaff laid a meaty hand on the gray's shoulder. "This is a fine horse; use him. Don't try coming after Claude Baines," Bickerstaff's voice was lowered, but the softness sounded all the more menacing.

"When I get ready, I'm going to kill Baines," Rollie said, leaving no room for argument.

"It's your life," Bickerstaff replied simply. "You've been warned." With a pat on the gray's shoulder, he walked out of the barn.

Rollie went to the door of the barn and watched the arrogant man walk up the street and disappear into the general store. Though fat, Bickerstaff still moved with surprising agility. A man like that would bear watching. He'd spoke his peace plan and simple and hadn't felt the need to stand around blustering afterwards. This was a man used to throwing his weight around and getting what he wanted.

Two of Bickerstaff's men were in the store when he entered. With a wave of his hand, Bickerstaff called one of them over to the corner. "Lang, I want you to keep an eye on that jasper, Dukes."

"Sure, Hank, is that him down by the stable?"

"That's him," Bickerstaff answered, taking a cracker from the barrel and slipping it into his mouth. "If he doesn't leave town in a few days, kill him!"

Morning came slowly to the town of Cordova and with the sun came a restless feeling of apprehension. The citizens hurried about their business careful not to look into each other's eyes. Each was afraid, and wondering who would be next.

Over the years, the town had survived a few Indian attacks and the robbery attempts of outlaws. These dangers were considered everyday hazards, but this was different. Cold blooded killings for no apparent reasons had them spooked. They didn't know who to trust or whom to suspect. The danger lurking in the shadows was wearing on the town.

In his room at the hotel, Rollie Dukes lay in his bed. The sun was streaming in through the window, and the room was already heating up. Rollie rolled in bed and stretched luxuriously. It was well past his usual hour of rising, but the bed was soft and felt good.

Rollie's eyes fell to his shirt, hanging on the bedpost and the badge that was pinned to it. The sight of the badge brought a frown to his face, he still wasn't sure he should have taken the job. But despite his misgivings, Rollie was intrigued.

He had seen a lot of killing in his time and there had always been a reason for it. Rollie was thinking there would be one here as well. Rollie thought if he knew the reason that someone was killed, he could figure out who could stand to gain.

Joshua Burke had raised the question that Hank Bickerstaff was behind the killings. Many of the town folks had been quick to agree, but Rollie wasn't so sure.

Bickerstaff was a man that Rollie could easily understand. Bickerstaff wouldn't hesitate to kill, if the situation demanded, but it would be face to face and out in the open. He was the type to walk hard heeled over anything in his way. Public opinion meant very little to him. He'd do his killing with no apologies.

Pushing that from his mind, Rollie climbed out of bed. Dressing slowly, Rollie considered where to start. That was part of the reason he had stayed in bed so long. Being new to law enforcement, Rollie found himself at a loss of how to proceed. A serious man by nature, Rollie rode for the brand and took his job very serious. In this case, the brand was represented by the town.

Jamming his hat on, Rollie went down the stairs. As usual, Sarah Eckles was on duty behind the desk. "Good morning Sheriff," she said sounding amused.

Rollie told her good morning, and started for the door. "Stage came in late last night," she commented, as Rollie stopped at the door. "Someone came in that you might want to talk with."

"Oh yeah, who was that?" Rollie asked absently. He was more concerned with the meeting that was taking place across the street. Charles Tinsworth was having a lengthy and serious discussion with Carney.

"Jim and Mort Killigan's niece, Rebecca Moreland," Sarah said, watching for a reaction. "I guess she's here to claim Jim's ranch."

"Nothing wrong with that, I guess," Rollie replied, wishing he could hear what Carney was telling Tinsworth. Whatever it was, it was pleasing the big banker.

Tinsworth smiled in pure satisfaction, and lit a cigar. Talking fast and using many gestures, Tinsworth issued instructions to Carney.

Whatever, he said to Carney; it built a fire under the gunslinger's tail, as he almost ran to his horse.

"Tell me about this feller, Tinsworth?" Rollie asked, gesturing out the window. "What's his deal?"

"Not much to tell really. He came to town and right away began acquiring things," Sarah said simply, but her tone told Rollie much more than her words.

"He had money when he came to town then?"

"Enough to buy the bank and a small ranch outside of town, but he didn't pay for everything."

"So that's why he has men like Carney on the payroll," Rollie commented, as much to himself as to the woman standing beside him.

"He never did anything that could be proved, but there was some strange disappearances and Tinsworth's men moved in on their claims. But of course, Bickerstaff has done the same thing."

Well that was no new story, most big ranchers started by pushing out the smaller homesteaders. Some people disapproved, but most just figured the land was for the taking. Whoever could latch onto it and hold it deserved it.

"How about Jim Killigan?" Rollie asked, watching Tinsworth return back to the bank.

"He and Mort were the first ones in this country. Mort went into the mountains looking for gold, but Jim started a ranch on the edge of the foothills. By the time the others came, he had a good sized operation and several tough cowboys," Sarah replied. Rollie could tell she really liked the two Killigan brothers.

"He must have been quite a man to have come out here then carved out a ranch, to say nothing of hanging onto it."

"Everyone seemed a little afraid of him, but I thought he was the nicest, kindest man I ever met."

"Evidently, someone wasn't afraid of him," Rollie commented dryly.

"That's why you should talk with his niece," Sarah paused and seemed to choose her words carefully. "She may not know what she's getting into," Sarah reminded him.

"I'll be over at the office, send her over when she wakes up," Rollie said, stepping out onto the boardwalk.

Before going over to the office, Rollie strolled around back, to examine the ground where Ben Riggs had been killed. The townspeople had trampled over the ground, but Rollie still went over it inch by inch. It was a maze of scuffed tracks, none of which offered any clues to the killer's identity. Rollie was about to give up when a smudge by the corner of the jail caught his eye. Bending down, Rollie studied the track, and scratched his jaw thoughtfully.

It was a moccasin track. Not many white men wore moccasins, not in this part of the country anyway. The Navajos were friendly, and the Apaches rarely came this far north.

Rising to his feet, Rollie looked around carefully. Making sure no one was watching. Rollie took the toe of his boot and wiped out the track. Rollie squatted down, his back to the jail, rolling a smoke.

Why would Ben be back here? This was just a walkway between the buildings, no reason to be here. Maybe he was going somewhere and this was the shortest route. Could be, but maybe the killer lured him back here. Be something to check on.

Course, Rollie didn't know the jailer's schedule, maybe he was just coming to work and this was the way he came. He should find out where Ben lived. If this was Ben's normal route, maybe the killer knew that and laid in wait for the old man.

Rollie glanced up and down the alley. Not likely, there just wasn't anywhere to hide. Ben could have seen the killer from a long ways away. If it was someone he had reason to fear, he wouldn't have walked right up to the man.

Ben Riggs knew his killer.

Aw crud, that wasn't surprising, Rollie decided. Cordova was a small place, everybody knew everybody.

Flipping his smoke away he wondered what the building behind the jail was. It was a huge building, over twice the size of the jail. Rollie made a note to find out what it was.

With a sigh, he walked around the jail. Whatever else the sheriff and Ben Riggs had been, they kept a neat place. Rollie dropped in a chair, slowly going through the desk. In the bottom drawer he found a small book.

Rollie licked his lips. He'd seen lots of books like this. Cattlemen carried them to make notes when they were riding the range. They wrote down grass conditions, which water holes were full, when cows dropped their calves stuff like that. Maybe a sheriff would carry such a book.

Excited Rollie cracked open the book. He placed his feet on the desk, leaning back in his chair as he read. It was the sheriff's book. Rollie paged through notations of fines. He stopped reading a note from the year before.

Some of Bickerstaff's cattle had gotten into Marge Ross' cornfield, destroying some of the crop. The sheriff had looked at the field, then ordered Bickerstaff to give Marge four head of cattle. The last notation said that Bickerstaff's foreman, Gene Lang had delivered the cattle to Marge three days later.

Rollie smiled, he was starting to like the sheriff. Still smiling, Rollie leafed through the book. Finally near the back, Rollie found a page with Jim Killigan written across the top. Excited Rollie scanned down through the page and quickly decided this was the sheriff's notes on the killing of Jim Killigan.

Dragging his feet off the desk, Rollie placed the book on the center of the desk, bending close and reading carefully. By the time he finished, Rollie knew the job had been done by a man who knew his business. One shot from over four hundred yards. That was a long shot that most men wouldn't even try.

Consulting the book, Rollie searched for a mention of the weapon used. All the book said was "large caliber rifle". The one thing that jumped out of the book at Rollie was the mention of the tracks. The sheriff had found a lot of tracks. For sure the killer had scouted the ranch for several days before settling on a spot to do his business.

Rollie tossed the book aside and leaned back in his chair. All along he'd had a sneaky suspicion that there were two killers operating in this area. Now he was sure of it.

Besides the differences in the weapons, Rollie figured the jasper that did in Ben Riggs could walk across a fresh snow drift without leaving any sign. He surely wouldn't have left tracks all around the Killigan ranch.

Pushing the daybook aside, Rollie resumed his search of the desk. He felt a little funny looking through another man's private things. Rollie stopped, glancing up at the ceiling. Surely the sheriff would want the killer found. Deciding he would, Rollie opened the bottom drawer of the desk. Folded neatly in the bottom was a huge hand-drawn map of the county. Below the map was a separate sheet of paper, listing all the land transactions for the county. Evidently, along with his other duties, the sheriff had served as the county assessor.

Feeling he might be onto something, Rollie spread the map out across the desk. The map was huge; it hung off the desk on all four sides. Looking at the map, several things became clear to Rollie. First of all, the sheriff had some talent when it came to drawing a map. The second thing Rollie saw, was the sheriff had been a meticulous man. He had painstakingly recorded everything on the sheet of paper. Records of every transaction was also duplicated on the map.

As he studied the map, Rollie whistled softly. Jim Killigan had been one smart man. Over the years, Killigan had managed to buy up quite a bit of land. Most big ranchers didn't actually own the land they used. They simply moved in and held the land by sheer force.

Killigan had been different. He had filed on the land where his headquarters sat. Mort had filed on the land right beside him and later Jim had bought the land from Mort. Early on it looked like Killigan had his men file on land, and then he had bought it from them after they proved up.

Rollie knew how that worked. After the Homestead Act was passed, a person could file a claim on a quarter section of land. If they built a house and lived on and worked the land for a year, then the land became theirs.

It was easy to see that Jim Killigan had directed his men on which parcels to file on. They had filed along a steam which bordered the north side of the ranch. Other parcels that Killigan obtained had lined the east and south borders of the ranch.

After the year, Jim Killigan had simply bought the land.

Smart man. With the mountains backing him up on the west, Killigan effectively controlled several thousand acres. More importantly he controlled the water. Anyone trying to file on parcels of land inside Killigan's ranch would be high and dry. No water.

Homesteaders were a thorn in the side of the big ranchers. Since the ranchers usually didn't own the land they claimed, a homesteader could file on it. By gaining ownership to a lot of his land, Jim Killigan had worked to control that problem.

As he studied the map, Rollie saw that Killigan hadn't been as successful as he would have liked. The homesteaders were moving in. They'd taken to filing on parcels which bordered the north side of Killigan's range.

Killigan, for all his planning had made a mistake, maybe a big one.

He'd filed his claims on the south side of the stream. If he would have filed on the north side, he might have been able to cut the homesteaders off from the water. Too late, Killigan must have seen his mistake. Of late he'd been acquiring a few parcels on the north side of the river.

Rollie sat down in the chair, rubbing his jaw. This was important. If the homesteaders were crowding Killigan, there would have been friction between the two parties.

Rollie had seen this many times before. It was the classic start to a range war. Big ranchers were claiming and using land they didn't actually own. But of course in their mind the land was rightfully theirs. And maybe it should be, but the farmers didn't see it that way.

Homesteaders from the east, hungry for land, moved in and filed claims. If they could hang on for a year, the land was theirs and the rancher was out. The rancher's response was almost always to hire fighters.

That's when the trouble started.

It usually started with threats. If threats didn't work, stock was killed, barns burned. If that didn't do the trick, then the fighters were sent to earn their pay. Sometimes the killings were out in the open and sometimes the homesteader would just disappear.

Maybe Killigan was threatening the homesteaders and one of them got mad enough to take a shot at Killigan.

Rollie had never heard of a homesteader killing a rancher. They were usually peaceful family men. Men just looking for a place of their own. Still it could have happened. Push a man hard enough and he'll do something.

What he needed to do was talk to one of the homesteaders. Maybe he could get a read on how tense the situation had been.

Rollie looked down at the map. A homesteader named Bud Swenson had the place closest to the Killigan headquarters.

Rollie folded up the map, replacing it in the drawer. Maybe he should go talk to Swenson. Rollie felt he might get a read on the mood of the homesteaders.

Bud Swenson? Dang! He'd heard that name. Where? Rollie leaned back closing his eyes. Where had he heard that name? That was the man Sarah had helped while his wife was sick.

Maybe he should go talk to Sarah. Find out about Swenson. Get a feel for the man.

Rollie smiled to himself. That was foolish. He didn't need to talk to Sarah. He could size up the man himself. Still it would be a fine excuse to talk to her. And Rollie realized, he wanted to talk to her.

Rollie was jolted out of his thoughts by the door opening. He looked up to see a very pretty young woman standing in the doorway. She used a delicate hand to push back a stray lock of long brown hair, and then looked at Rollie with a pair of cool gray eyes. "Are you the sheriff?"

"Yes ma'am, Rollie Dukes," Rollie said, snapping to his feet. "And you would be?" he asked, extending his hand across the desk.

"Rebecca Moreland," she answered, ignoring his hand as she slid gracefully into a chair. "Jim Killigan was my uncle."

Frowning slightly, Rollie let his hand drop and sank back into his own chair. "I've been meaning to hunt you up and have a talk," Rollie admitted.

"Good," Rebecca said, clutching her small purse in her lap. "I wish to take possession of my uncle's ranch. Are you the man I see about that?"

Rollie frowned, his experience in these types of matters were slim as a piece of jack rabbit jerky. He scratched is head. "Did your uncle leave a will?"

"No, I don't believe so, but he always meant for me to have the ranch after he was gone," Rebecca replied primly.

"I take it you and Mort were his only kin?"

"That's right. My mother has been dead for years and Uncle Jim never married."

Rollie shrugged and slapped the top of the desk lightly with both hands. "Well, I reckon I can ride out and have a pow wow with

Mort. If he doesn't have any objections, you move right in," Rollie decided.

A slight frown marred Rebecca's pretty face, "How long will that take?"

"I don't know, a day or two."

Rebecca Moreland nodded crisply and started to rise, then sank back down. "Have you apprehended the man who killed my uncle?"

"I just started this job last night," Rollie explained.

Her expression severe, Rebecca looked across the desk. "That's an excuse I suppose," she admitted, standing up. "But I warn you, I expect results," she said haughtily. With a swish of her skirts, she turned and pranced out the door.

As the door closed, Rollie tipped his chair back and rubbed his jaw. Quite a woman, he reflected. Young, but already a head for business. Rollie hadn't missed the fact that she inquired about the ranch before her uncle.

Rollie dearly wanted to go through the daybook some more, but he regretfully pocketed it and headed down to the stable. First thing was to have that talk with Bud Swenson, and then go see Mort Killigan. Rollie wanted to get the matter of who was to inherit Jim Killigan's ranch out of the way. Besides, Mort might know something about all the killings.

Those old prospectors moved around a lot, and they knew a lot more of what went on than most folks would guess. Problem was going to be finding the old sourdough. A body looking for gold wouldn't advertise where they found it. Not if they were wishful of keeping it.

Rumor had it that old Mort sure enough found gold, but nobody knew where. A few had tried following Mort, but he had always given them the slip. Now, Rollie wasn't buying all that nonsense about a gold mine. In Rollie's experience, folks would always believe every rumor about gold, because they wanted a share of it.

Pushing Mort and his gold from his mind, Rollie left the jail, crossing over to the hotel. As he walked, Rollie could feel his heart pounding in his chest. It seemed like his heart was hammering louder than his boots thumping on the boardwalk.

He felt himself grinning. There was something about that girl that made him feel jumpy, like he'd swallowed a bucket of crickets.

He managed to wipe the silly grin off his face before he pushed through the door of the hotel. Sarah was there, working at her counter, looking pretty as a sunrise. She glanced up as he pushed through the door. Rollie could see the curiosity in her eyes, along with a flash of disapproval in the quick frown which sprang to her lips. All of a sudden, Rollie was wishing he hadn't come. This was foolish. She probably thought he should be out working, instead of being in here. "Sheriff," she said coolly.

"Ma'am," Rollie replied, sweeping the hat off his head. "I was wondering if I could ask you a few questions."

"Why? Am I in trouble?" she asked, the hint of laughter tugging at the corners of her mouth.

All of a sudden the room seemed small and awfully hot. Rollie stepped back, rubbing the back of his neck. "Aw, no, ma'am. I was wanting to ask you a few questions about a feller named Bud Swenson."

"Mister Swenson? You surely don't think he's mixed up in all of this?"

"No ma'am. I mean I don't know." Rollie took a deep breath, trying to calm his racing mind and galloping heart. "I need to talk to him, and I heard you helped him out a while back. I was hoping you could tell me what kind of feller he is."

Sarah flashed him a smile which made his knees feel like gravy. "Why, sheriff, were you asking about me?"

"No, no, I just heard it in passing," Rollie stammered, feeling his face burn red.

Sarah laughed. "Okay, then. What do you want to know about Mister Swenson?"

Rollie twisted his hat in his hands, trying to get his thoughts back on track. "Well, I was noticing that over the last few years there's been a lot of homesteaders claiming land right up against Jim Killigan's ranch. Now, it's been my experience that big ranchers don't care for that much. I was thinking that if Killigan was leaning on them homesteaders, maybe one of them didn't take kindly to it."

"You think Mister Swenson killed Mister Killigan?"

"Oh no, I was just gonna talk to him. See if there was some hard feelings between the homesteaders and Killigan. I was gonna ask you if you thought he would talk to me. If he thought one of his neighbors killed Killigan, would he be the type to say, or would he keep it to himself?"

"I think he would," Sarah said gravely. "I think he would tell you if he killed Mister Killigan." Sarah laughed, a quick, merry sound. "The thought of Bud Swenson killing someone is laughable. When I was out there his wife told me that when they had fried chicken, she had to kill the chicken. He's a little squeamish."

Rollie nodded. "So he'll talk to me?"

"I believe he will, but I can tell you, you are on the wrong track."

"Why is that?"

"Because Mister Killigan didn't hate the farmers. He helped them. He told me."

"Really? He told you that?"

Sarah nodded. "Mister Killigan said they were good people, just looking for a chance to get ahead, like the rest of us."

"Maybe, they are good folks," Rollie admitted, "But I recall a story about being a rotten apple in every barrel. I best go talk to them."

A few minutes later as he rode away from Cordova, Rollie considered what Sarah had told him. He didn't necessarily believe it. Not that he thought Sarah lied to him. Far from it. Instead, he figured Killigan lied to her.

Men, even old timers like Killigan liked to impress a pretty girl like Sarah. Killigan wouldn't say he was burning out the farmers. Didn't mean he was, but it didn't prove he wasn't either.

Rollie was still mulling it over when he rode up to the Swenson place. It was a nice place, backed up to a small stream. A narrow road cut the center of the place, leading back to a house and barn. On one side of the road was a field of wheat and on the other a stand of hay.

Rollie saw a ditch that had been dug to divert water from the stream to the fields. The ditch was dry of water, but judging from the mud in the bottom it had carried water recently.

As he rode closer Rollie saw a rider confronting the family in a large vegetable garden between the house and barn. Rollie felt a hot flash of anger as he recognized the rider. It was Carney.

"You should take some good advice," Carney was saying as he leered down at the Swenson family. "You got a nice family here.

You sure wouldn't want anything to happen to them." Carney shook his head. "Yes, sir, be a downright shame."

Whatever else Carney might have said was cut off as Rollie slapped the spurs to the gray horse. Sensing the threat behind him, Carney started to turn, his hand sweeping for his gun. Carney was fast and he was pulling the gun free when Rollie dove from the saddle. Rollie slammed into the smaller man, wiping him clean out of the saddle.

They hit the ground with a thud. Carney squirming to get away and Rollie wildly raining punches, trying for the knockout shot. His face streaming blood from a cut over his eye, Carney rolled away, snatching up the gun he'd dropped. Scrambling to his feet, Rollie slapped the gun away with his left hand and swatted Carney's face with his right.

Growling, Rollie drove the smaller man to the ground with four hammering punches. As Carney tried to roll into a ball, Rollie grabbed him up by the shirt. Jerking him off the ground, Rollie slammed him into the wooden fence.

Pushing his forearm across Carney's throat, Rollie leaned in close. "Tell your boss, he tries this again and I will kill him," Rollie hissed.

Without waiting for a reply, Rollie spun around slinging Carney in the direction of his horse. "You give Tinsworth the message, and then you get on your horse and ride. I ever see you again and I will shoot you down on the spot."

For a second, Carney looked like he was going to bluster, but then he whirled away, stalking to his horse. He swung into the saddle, glaring down at Rollie. "This ain't over."

Rollie laughed and scooped Carney's pistol off the ground. He held the gun out to Carney. "Don't forget your gun."

Carney took the gun. He licked his lips, staring at the gun in his hand. He glanced up at Rollie, then back down at the gun. "Go ahead. Try it," Rollie taunted.

A tick jumped on Carney's cheek, as he wrestled with his nerve. Suddenly, he spun his horse and rode away.

Blowing out a deep sigh, Swenson stepped up. "Thanks, Mister," he said holding out his hand and shaking his head. "I ain't sure but what you been chewing on loco weed, but I want to shake your hand."

"He wasn't gonna try anything," Rollie replied, taking the hand. "We've met before."

Swenson nodded. "I heard. You'd be Dukes, then. What can I do for you?"

Rollie tapped the badge on his chest. "I'm looking into the murder of Jim Killigan."

Swenson frowned, glancing quickly back at his family. "Abby, why don't you take the kids into the house?" He waited a beat, while his wife gathered the kids. "Why don't we walk over to the barn? Kids don't need to hear about all this."

"Sure," Rollie agreed, gathering the reins and leading the gray down to the barn.

"I don't know what I can tell you about Jim's death," Swenson said, as Rollie loosened the cinch and let the gray drink from the trough. "I didn't even hear about Jim being killed till a couple days afterward."

"Okay," Rollie said, choosing his words carefully. "I was looking at a map the sheriff had and I noticed a lot of homesteaders have filed right up next to Killigan's range. I was thinking maybe Killigan tried something like Carney just did and one of you folks decided to do something about it."

Swenson was smiling and shaking his head before Rollie even finished. "I can see where you might think that, but it wasn't that way."

Rollie frowned. "How was it?"

"Jim was a good man. Smart too," Bud said. "He helped me pick this place."

"Why would he do that?"

Swenson grinned a little. "He had plans."

Rollie swore to himself and rolled his eyes. Getting information outta this fella was like pulling teeth. "What plans?"

Swenson hesitated, picking up a stick. He turned the stick in his hands looking down at the stream. Finally, he snapped the stick, tossing it away. "I'm gonna tell you something, but you gotta keep it under your hat."

"Okay, tell me, I won't say a word."

Swenson nodded. "See Jim was a man who looked to the future. Years ago, when Jim laid out his spread, he was already thinking ahead." Rollie nodded, he knew that from looking at the map. Bud nodded his head at the stream. "This creek takes a turn south and cuts in besides Jim's house."

Rollie followed Swenson's pointing finger with his eyes and could see where the stream took a gentle turn. 'Okay," he grunted, not at all sure what that had to do with anything.

Bud spun on his heel, pointing to the west. "Now from here, the river runs pretty much east and west, going all the way back to the mountains. This made a good border for the north side of Jim's range. When us homesteaders started coming into this country, Jim would encourage all of us to file on parcels on the north side of the creek."

"Why would he do that?" Rollie wondered out loud.

"I'm getting to that," Swenson said with a smile. "See Jim would help us file and after the year was up and if a feller wanted to move on, Jim would buy the land. That happened a couple of times, but mostly folks stayed. We have a good deal here."

"How so?"

"Jim would let us run a few cows in with his herd. We could start with ten and his hands took care of them. Come roundup time we would come over and claim our calves. Each year Jim would let us keep one female to increase our cow herd and one male to fatten up. The rest of our calves, Jim would buy."

"Folks liked that?"

"Sure," Bud replied quickly. "What's not to like? We get to run some cattle have a fat steer to butcher every year, and sell our calves for cash money. It was a great deal for us."

"What did Killigan get in return?" Rollie asked.

Swenson gestured to his massive vegetable garden. "I gave him stuff out of the garden. Several others did too. Kerrigan who has four milk cows gave him some milk and Smitty who keeps a mess of chickens would take over eggs, and from time to time a fryer. Everybody did something like that." Swenson paused. "But the main thing was Jim owned five parcels of land on this side of the river. We were to pitch in and farm four of them for him."

"Smart," Rollie grunted. "But why keep it a secret?"

"I don't know, but that wasn't all of it."

"Okay," Rollie said, feeling impatience spurring him.

"See when Jim hatched this plan; he brought a surveyor from back east. He had this surveyor lay out the plots, each one an even quarter section."

"Made it easy on you fellas," Rollie observed.

"Sure did, but Jim also showed us how to double up our land."

"Oh yeah," Rollie said, wondering where this was going. "How did he do that?"

"You know the rules. Each person can file on a parcel. Long as he builds a house and works the ground for a year it's his."

Bud grinned a little sheepishly. "Guess this ain't exactly legal, but who's gonna care, there's a lot of land." Bud blew out a sigh, his conscious eased. "Jim talked to the sheriff and they had a little deal. See I filed on this parcel," he said pointing to the barn. "My wife, she filed on this one," he added waving to the house. He laughed a little. "We are standing on the dividing line right now. House is on one parcel, barn on the other. After the year the sheriff comes out to see if we proved up, and as long as there is a building on both parcels and the ground is being worked, he don't look too hard at the buildings."

"So that's the big secret?" Rollie asked shaking his head. "That ain't much. I think I heard it being done before."

"Well that's part of it. There's more. Did you see the irrigation ditch when you rode in?" he asked and Rollie nodded. "When Jim had his surveyor out here, he surveyed the ditches. There's twenty in all. Each one has a number one through five. We got a system. Ones get water on Monday, twos on Tuesday and so on."

"That way the creek doesn't run dry," Rollie said following the system.

"Sure, Jim's cows got to get water from the creek."

"Your cows too. If they are running with his," Rollie said, and Bud nodded. "So all the farms get water once a week? How well does that work?"

"Worked pretty good," Bud said, beaming as he waved an arm at his fields. "Wouldn't you say?"

Rollie could tell the man was proud of his crops, so he took a look, even though Rollie really didn't care. "Looks real good,"

Rollie replied, and he wasn't lying, the man had an excellent stand of hay and a good looking wheat crop.

"You just bet it does," Bud chattered, beaming like a new papa. He grinned at Rollie. "Which brings us to the next part. You remember how I said Jim had five parcels and we farmed four of them for him?"

"Yeah, I remember that."

"Well on that last quarter, we're gonna build a mill."

"A mill? Like a flour mill?"

"Yeah, flour and feed grain too. Jim done some figuring. He said it took him three years to raise a calf to where he could sell it for beef. He thought that if he fed them grain and hay through the winter he could trim a year off that. He said if a person ground the grain, it was better for the cows."

"So why keep it a secret?"

"Well everything wasn't quite legal, the claiming of the land and all." Bud laughed. "Word around is that for as many parcels as Jim was able to buy, he musta had a hundred men working for him. I heard that some of his guys got a new name every year. Guy was Bob Smith one year when he was filing a claim and Bob Jones the next year."

Rollie nodded, he'd heard of that being done before. "So what? It ain't quite on the up and up but it's been done. Doesn't look like it would raise many eyebrows."

"Maybe not, but Jim was trying to get the government to sell him the rest of the land he was using on his ranch. He petitioned the Governor. Jim thought he'd get the okay this summer."

"Why would they do that?" Rollie asked. "Is that legal?"

"Sure it is, land belongs to the government, and they can do what they want. Jim was an important man in these parts; Governor would want him on his side. Besides the way Jim explained it, he told the Governor he could make sure all of us would vote for him."

"Would you have?"

"If Jim said to, sure. But it weren't just us farmers; everybody had a stake in this. See those two parcels? They belong to Moser and his wife. I just worked out a deal to farm it for them for shares. Hartshorn and his missus have a couple parcels back yonder, I heard Smitty is gonna work them. Most of the town has parcels out here.

That's a pile of votes." Bud grinned. "Course I reckon the Governor got a little pocket change to boot."

Rollie paced, looking off towards the stream. "Seems like you and Killigan talked quite a bit."

Swenson shrugged. "Sure we talked some, he used to come by, and he'd stay for supper sometimes. I think he was lonely."

"Smart guy though," Rollie said. "He sure had a lot of plans."

All of a sudden the humor drained off Swenson's face, and he misted up like a spring morning. "Yeah, sure is a shame it'll probably fall apart now. Dang shame."

"So we find who killed him," Rollie said savagely. "You seem like a smart guy, you must have some thoughts on who would have done this."

"I don't know," Swenson said, with a sad shake of his head. "I've thought about it till my head hurt. Me and the missus talked it over some." Swenson finished with a shrug.

"Nothing? No ideas at all?"

"Well there was one thing, doesn't seem like much."

"What is it?"

"The mill, we were supposed to start building it a few weeks before Jim died, but he decided to wait."

"Something scare him off?"

"Didn't seem like that. He didn't seem scared at all. He just said we'd have to wait."

"Maybe he had a reason. Like a business reason?" Rollie wondered.

Swenson was already shaking his head. "I don't think so. See we was set to start on the silos. We are going to be harvesting our wheat in a few weeks. We need those silos to store the grain."

"You weren't gonna start on the mill itself?"

"Naw that was set for this winter. No big rush on that, but the silos we are gonna be needing them soon. Harvest time comes, gotta have a place to put the grain."

"So maybe he was scared," Rollie said, getting a little excited. This could be something. "Maybe somebody warned him off."

Swenson shrugged, and Rollie could tell, the farmer wasn't convinced. "Jim didn't seem the type to run scared. Mostly he did what he pleased. Didn't worry about folks much."

"Maybe it was a hang up on supplies. How do you build a silo anyway?"

"We were going to use mud bricks. Adobe. Jim had a place we were gonna make the bricks. Me and Kline we went over and built the kiln for baking the bricks, then all of a sudden Jim says stop."

"He give a reason?"

Swenson scuffed his toe. "He said the mud wasn't good clay. That it wouldn't hold."

"You didn't agree?" Rollie pressed, seeing the hesitation in the man.

"Aw, I don't know. I mean Jim was a smart man, way smarter than me, and if he said the mud was no good, I gotta believe him."

"But you don't?"

Bud blew out a sigh, looking away from Rollie. "Looked good to me."

Rollie rode away from the Swenson place thinking about the mill. Why would Killigan stop construction on the mill? Didn't make any kind of sense.

One thing was for certain, Killigan had thought things through. He'd found a way to use the homesteaders instead of fighting them. Rollie would bet Killigan had spent years planning this. Refining it. Down to the last detail.

Rollie frowned. So Killigan spends years planning this thing, and then at the last minute realizes the mud won't make good bricks. Not hardly.

Rollie let the gray have his head, while he pondered the problem. There was no way Jim Killigan had left the making of the bricks to chance. Rollie would bet he'd checked that clay more than a few times. Besides, Swenson thought the mud was good.

So why stop the mill?

Somebody had scared him off.

Pure and simple. That had to be it.

Question was who?

Maybe old Mort would have an idea about that. Now, he just had to find Mort.

Now in his day, Rollie had done a little prospecting, so as he rode away from the Swenson farm, he checked off the likely places to start. East and south weren't likely, that was open country. It had been Rollie's experience that gold was found in rough, broken country. North? Maybe, but Rollie had a hunch west was the proper direction to take.

Rollie rode the rest of the day and as evening set in; he was ready to give up on his task. Finding Mort was not going to be easy and Rollie hated to be away from town for too long. He was about to swing the gray around and head back to town when he heard the sound of a rifle being cocked behind him.

CHAPTER FOUR

Harley Harper rode slowly, he was dead tired, but he was also confused. He shook his head in disgust. This was supposed to be his corner of the range to patrol. Normally Harley wouldn't see another soul or even the sign of another human. Today was certainly different. Seemed like he was up to his neck in folks.

Yesterday, just at dark he'd seen the tracks where ten or twelve head of Bickerstaff's cattle had drifted onto Killigan's range. This morning he'd left the line shack early to bring them back. Before leaving, he'd left orders for his so-called helper, Claude Baines, to go clean out a waterhole south and east of the line shack.

Tumbleweeds had blown in the waterhole and in time they would catch even more weeds and debris. Left like it was the weeds could plug up the inlet or even rot and spoil the water.

Thinking about it, Harley scowled and swore under his breath. It was something Baines should have caught and taken care of on his own. After all, that was the man's job. He took care of that part of the range. Horace would have caught it. A wave of sadness swept over him. Harley and Horace had worked together for a good long time. Even back before they went to work for Bickerstaff.

When the trouble first started and the gun hands moved in, Horace had wanted to quit and move on. He'd heard there was good jobs out west in California.

It was Harley who talked Horace into staying. They had worked a long time for Bickerstaff, and it felt like home here. They went to Hank with their concerns and Hank had moved them out to the line shack, promising them that they could work the cattle in peace. That the fighting wouldn't come to them.

Now Horace was dead, shot in the back, and Harley was saddled with that idiot Claude Baines. For a few days Harley thought that Baines was simply lazy, but after today Harley was wondering if there wasn't something more sinister at work.

After sending Baines to clean the waterhole, Harley had set about to trail the cattle. The trail was several days old, but Harley could have followed it in his sleep. They were headed west and moving right along. Harley found them all the way over at Diablo Canyon, spread out in a nice piece of bottom land.

Now, by then Harley was totally confused and more than a little mad.

These cattle hadn't drifted this far, they had been driven.

Even if he hadn't seen the tracks, Harley would have known the cattle were driven. Cattle wouldn't just travel several miles in one day for no good reason. Cattle might drift along in front of a storm, but it had been dry dust for weeks. They had been driven.

And Harley knew by whom.

He'd spotted the tracks of the rider pushing the cattle even though the rider had taken pains to hide his tracks. At times he had ridden right behind the cows, hoping to mix his tracks in with the cattle at other times, he'd ridden off to the side. It was a weak attempt, but it might have worked if Harley hadn't been wondering why the cattle would move so far so fast. It might have worked, but it didn't, he'd seen the tracks, and what's more, he recognized them. The bay horse that Claude Baines rode.

Scratching his head, over what Baines was up to, Harley had done some exploring. It quickly became clear why Baines was getting no work done. It wasn't because he was lazy, it was because he was spending his time over around Diablo Canyon.

What he was doing here, Harley didn't have the foggiest notion. Baines was riding back and forth, like he was riding a patrol, or like he was looking for something.

Then Harley cut across the tracks of Gene Lang. Harley had worked with Lang for years. He hadn't particularly liked Lang, but they had worked together. Harley easily recognized the tracks of Pogo, Lang's favorite horse. Harley swore and pushed back his hat.

So Lang had also been in this area as well? Why? Harley saw where Gene had met with someone, more than once. Again, why?

Why would Lang come all the way out here to meet someone?

Seemed like there would be only one answer to that. He wanted to keep the meeting a secret. Which didn't seem right to Harley,

Now driving the cattle back onto Bickerstaff's range, Harley was troubled. Something was going on here. Something not right.

Once he had the cattle safely back on Bickerstaff's range, Harley cut north towards the main house. He'd tell Hank what was going on, let him decide what to do. Harley blew out a sigh, maybe Horace had been right, and maybe it was time to move on.

Harley stretched in the saddle. He'd covered some miles today. If he would have agreed to leave when Horace wanted to, his friend would still be alive.

Harley heard the shot, but it didn't sound like a shot, it sounded like a clap of thunder. He felt the bullet smash through him, burning like a bolt of lightning. And in a vague, fuzzy way, he felt the ground as he thumped into it.

"You just sit real still, young feller," a cold voice called out.

Rollie could hear scuffling behind him, then the voice called out again. "Okay now, you swing down and face that gray," the voice said, then added with a touch of dry humor. "I'm telling you straight up, I ain't up to planting you, so if I have to kill you, I'm just gonna leave you where you hit the ground."

His face burning with embarrassment, Rollie swung down, and leaned his head against the saddle. Cursing himself for being so careless, Rollie listened to the sound of approaching footsteps. He was hoping this was Mort Killigan. From what he heard, Mort was a reasonable man. Despite the fact that he was half expecting it, Rollie still flinched when he felt the cold muzzle of the gun press into the small of his back. A dry chuckle rattled out of the man behind him. "Nothing like a Spencer to make a man pucker." He cackled, slipping Rollie's pistols from their holsters. "Okay, sonny boy, you can turn around now."

Slowly, Rollie let his hands fall as he turned to face his captor. What he saw was a slim, wiry man of about fifty years. Cold, blue eyes stared at Rollie with a measuring look, and there was no sign of warmth in the sun-burnt face.

The old man wrinkled his nose and spat in the dirt. "What's your name?" he asked, keeping the black muzzle of the rifle trained on Rollie's stomach.

Rollie had to swallow a few times, before he could even think about answering. His throat was dry, and he couldn't tear his eyes away from that rifle. A Spencer 56. Rollie felt a queasy, greasy feeling shoot through his guts. That rifle could blow a hole through a mud house.

An indignant look swept across the old man's face and he jabbed Rollie with the rifle. "Believe I asked you a question," he reminded with a voice cold enough to frost over a glass of whiskey.

"Name's Rollie Dukes."

Those blue eyes narrowed a mite and the muzzle of the rifle came up a fraction. "Rollie Dukes, eh? Seems, I heard tell of you. Can't say it was all good, but I never thought you would be a claim jumper."

"I'm not," Rollie tried to protest, but it came out a bit weak. Now as he said before, Rollie could, at times be a mean and impatient man, but a Spencer rifle buried in his guts tended to give a man the patience of Jobe. Right then Rollie was finding it hard to get too riled, in fact he was feeling down right friendly. "I'm looking for a man named Mort Killigan. That you?"

Fury swept across the old man's face, as he poked the rifle into the pit of Rollie's stomach. Rollie tried to back up a step, but he was pressed into that gray horse. The gray calmly munched at the dry grass, totally unconcerned with the crazy actions of humans. Baring his teeth in a snarl, the old man leaned into the rifle. "What you want with Mort? You looking to kill him?"

"No," Rollie denied quickly, wondering if the crazy old goat was trying to push that rifle clean through him. "I'm the new sheriff in town. I came out here to talk law business."

"Yeah? What kind of law business?"

"That's between me and Mort. If that's you, then put away that rifle and let's talk. If not, then I'll tell it to Mort when I find him."

The old man growled and spat on the ground. "Why you danged fool, I'm Mort Killigan. Now state your business fore I lose all patience and just blast you."

"Your niece is in town. She's laying claim to your brother's ranch."

For a second Mort's expression didn't flicker and he didn't move. Rollie wasn't sure, but he thought he could detect a hint of sadness in the old man. Finally, Mort eased the hammer down on the Spencer and tipped the rifle back over his shoulder. "Don't be getting no notions," Mort warned, patting the rifle. He took a step back squatting on his heels, looking off into the distance. "So, Becky's in town? Don't that beat all?" he asked, and for a man who hadn't seen his niece in a long time, he didn't sound overjoyed.

"Yeah, and she wants your brother's ranch."

Mort nodded absently. "Course she does." He rocked back and forth on his heels a few times and then sprang to his feet. "I got a camp over yonder. Come on. I'll fix us a mess of grub," the old man offered.

A little perplexed, Rollie gathered the gray's reins and followed the old prospector. As they walked, Mort passed the twin Smith and Wessons back to Rollie. "Don't be getting any fancy pants ideas," he warned, patting the Spencer.

Mort led the way to a bluff which shouldered fifty feet above the prairie floor. He took a faint game trail up the side of the bluff. Suddenly, they wove between two huge boulders and popped out on a grassy bench. The bench was small, maybe thirty yards long and half as wide. Just enough room for a camp and a few horses. An excellent place for a camp, invisible from below, the bench provided an excellent view of the surrounding country, including the waterhole.

"Good place," Rollie commented, turning the gray loose to graze with Mort's two horses.

"Came on it by accident," Mort admitted, stirring up a small fire. He sat a coffee pot on the edge of the fire then looked up at Rollie. "So you're Rollie Dukes?" he muttered and Rollie nodded. Mort cocked his head to one side, studying Rollie. "I knew Joe Turner," he said, a bit of a challenge in his voice.

Rollie grimaced and felt a twist in his guts. "I didn't know what I was getting into," he said quietly.

Mort nodded absently. "Reckon you'd been just a sprout when all that happened."

"Sixteen," Rollie said. "I came here looking for Claude Baines."

"Oh yeah? Claude's in these parts?"

"Working for Bickerstaff."

Mort nodded slowly, digesting the news. "Makes sense. Baines and Gene Lang are old riding buddies from way back."

Gene Lang? Rollie had heard that name but wasn't placing it. "Who's Lang?"

"Bickerstaff's foreman. Gene's a first rate cowman, but I heard he's better with a gun than cows. What about Baines? What you aiming to do? Kill him?"

"That was my thought."

"Nobody'll miss him, but won't change things. What's done is done. Doubt if killing him will even make you feel any better," Mort said, looking intently at Rollie. The old man shook his head, and then stood up, slapping his hands on his thighs. "So about the ranch. I'd like to have a talk with Becky fore you just turn it over to her."

"Sounds reasonable," Rollie said, still thinking about Claude Baines, Joe Turner and that wet night many years ago.

"I got a couple of things to clear up, then I'll be in town. Tomorrow, next day at the latest. Then we can set down with Becky and get her fixed up all legal like."

Rollie nodded, glad to have that detail out of the way. "Seen any strangers lately?" he asked casually.

A sly smile crept across Mort's weathered face. "You mean like the gent that's been sending folks off to meet their maker?" he asked and Rollie nodded. The smile melted off Mort's face as he shook his head. "No, and I been looking. I find the jasper that shot Jim, well, me and him is going to have a right serious chat."

"If I was you, I'd go careful. I got a notion there's more than one," Rollie warned.

"That don't hardly figure," Mort protested, but Rollie could see the old prospector mulling the idea over. He cocked his head off to one side, rolling the idea through his mind. Rollie kept still, letting the old timer think it through. Mort dug out a skillet, setting it on the fire. "Two, huh?" he grunted, pulling some bacon from his pack.

"That's the way I figure it," Rollie said, watching the old man carve strips of bacon and toss them in the skillet. Right then, Rollie made up his mind; he was going to trust Mort. "You know anybody who wears moccasins?"

"Yeah, a whole passel of Indians," Mort said, snorting out a laugh. When Rollie didn't laugh, Mort turned serious. "I reckon you're talking about a white man. Well, I don't know of one of them," he said, a question in his voice.

"I'm pretty sure the man that killed Ben Riggs was wearing moccasins," Rollie supplied.

His face clouding up, Mort swore bitterly, banging his knife off the skillet. "They kilt ol' Ben? Now why in the name of Harriet's hash would anybody want to go and do that?"

Rollie only shrugged, he'd been racking his brain for an answer to that one himself and didn't have a clue. Mort had a notion though. "You reckon the sheriff got onto something, and that's why they killed him, then maybe they got to thinking the sheriff said something to Ben?" Mort asked, as he forked the bacon onto two metal plates.

Rollie had started to pour up some coffee, now his hand froze over the cups. "It has crossed my mind," he admitted.

"It's a likely thought, only thing that really makes sense," Mort said.

Rollie blew out a sigh, filling the cups. "I need to do some looking into that."

"Feller tried to follow me the other day," Mort commented, passing a plate to Rollie.

Something in Mort's tone caught Rollie's attention. "Someone tried to follow you to your claim?"

"Maybe, but it didn't seem like that," Mort paused, trying to find a handle on the words to explain. "This was different."

Rollie had an idea what Mort meant. A man alone in the wilderness developed a feeling for the things around him. A wise man learned to trust these feelings.

"This jasper, he was different than most. Mostly when somebody tries to trail me to my claim, they hang way back, hoping I won't spot them. This yahoo kept trying to close up on me."

"Like he was working in close enough to take a shot at you?" Rollie asked around a mouthful of bacon.

Mort shot him a stiff smile. "Now that thought did cross my mind. I sure did contemplate doubling back and stretching his hide, but things being the way they was, I figured I'd best just give him the slip."

Rollie smiled, shooting the old prospector a sly look. "He was getting a little too close to your claim?"

"Something like that," Mort said, flatly, closing the subject.

Rollie didn't press; he knew how crotchety these old dust miners could be about their claims. Rollie had no interest in Mort's claim, but the old timer would never believe that. They ate in silence for a while, each man lost in his own thoughts.

It was Mort who broke the silence. "That hombre that trailed me, I figure he's the one that shot my brother," Mort said, topping off their coffee cups.

"What makes you say that?"

"A few days after I gave him the slip, I wandered back over there and done some snooping. Now, I'd already been out to Jim's ranch after he was killed and I found some tracks. They wasn't the same hoss, but it was the same as the fella dogging my trail."

Rollie got up and walked to the edge of the bench, looking across the plains, at the mountains glowing red in the setting sun. "Any chance that someone could have a grudge against your family?"

"Maybe, I suppose, but I couldn't guess why," Mort answered with a shrug.

"Well, your brother did have the best ranch around, and word has it that you hit it big."

Mort laughed and avoided the issue. "Folks sure do like to flap their gums. That's why I avoid them."

"Do you think your niece could be in any danger?"

Mort thought about that then shook his head. "No, I'm real certain Becky's out of danger."

Rollie swirled the coffee in his cup. "Do you know anything about your brother building a flour mill?"

Mort grinned, cocking his head. "You sure do get around. Must gossip more than a ladies sewing circle," Mort said, then added. "Yeah, Jim told me about that. He always had big plans."

"Was Jim having trouble with the homesteaders?"

"Naw, Jim kinda liked them and danged if he didn't find a way for them to help him," A wistful smile snuck onto the old man's face. "He was like that even when we were kids. Always thinking and plotting."

Rollie nodded. "I talked to Bud Swenson. He said they were all set to start on the mill, but then Jim said wait."

Mort scowled, his eyes drifting off into the distance. "Can't think why he would do that. Last time I talked to Jim he was in a sweat to get that mill built."

"Jim was trying to keep the mill a secret. Any idea why?"

Mort smiled waving his hand, "Aw that was just Jim. He liked keeping things quiet, then springing them on folks. See one thing Jim hated was looking like a fool, so he kept things quiet, till he knew they was gonna work. If they didn't work," Mort chuckled dryly, "Well, nobody ever heard about those."

Rollie scratched his chin, mulling it over. He wasn't sure he believed that. He glanced at the old timer, but Mort wasn't giving anything away. "Do you think the mill coulda been what got him killed?"

Mort poked the fire with his knife. "I don't rightly think so. I mean I doubt if either Hank or that slop bucket Tinsworth would be happy about it, but it wouldn't be a killing thing."

Mort flipped his knife, sticking it in the dirt. "See Hank and Tinsworth sure weren't happy about all the nesters moving into the country, but Jim was keeping them outta their hair."

"So why do you think he was killed?"

A sad look settling on his weathered, hound-dog face. Mort shook his head. "I don't know," he rasped, his voice sounding like a raw wound. He pulled his knife from the ground and stuck it into his belt. "But you can bet your bonnet, I mean to find out." Mort kicked dirt over the fire. "I'm gonna turn in, you're welcome to stay the night."

With that he spread his blanket on the ground. Rollie followed suit, but sleep would not come. Mort knew more than he was saying.

Rollie couldn't guess why the old man would hold back, but he was. Rollie could feel it.

Dawn was breaking when Rollie awoke. Pulling on his boots, Rollie glanced over to where Mort slept. The old prospector was gone!

Dropping his boot, Rollie snatched a pistol from the holster. With one boot on, Rollie eased over to where Mort had slept.

Running an experienced eye over the ground, Rollie could tell what happened as easily as if he saw it happen. No signs of a struggle, so Mort had left on his own free will. He'd been pretty quiet not to have awakened Rollie. The sheriff could see the dents in the ground where the old prospector knelt to roll his bedroll. Mort had carried his saddle and packs away from the camp, and then returned for his horse and mule.

His curiosity satisfied, Rollie returned to his own bedroll. Swiftly, he finished dressing and packed his gear. Rollie dearly wanted a cup of coffee, but decided it could wait until he got back to town.

Rollie saddled the gray and led the big horse down out of the hollow. Swinging into the saddle, Rollie looked thoughtfully in the direction Mort Killigan had taken.

Rollie had no intentions of following the old prospector. Chances were, that the old coot was hunkered down behind a rock somewhere just waiting to see if Rollie would follow. Rollie knew if he tried to tail the old prospector, he'd likely get a couple of those fifty-six caliber slugs for his trouble.

The gray fought at the bit, eager to be going, so Rollie turned him toward town. The gray set out at a rolling lope, which Rollie knew could eat up the miles in a hurry.

As the gray covered ground, Rollie looked for signs of minerals. This didn't look like gold country to the sheriff, but it surely must be.

Mort's claim had to be close by. Nothing else would explain the old prospectors' actions this morning. Rollie shook his head; it would be a miserable job to pan the gold. There didn't look to be enough water in this whole country to pan more'n a couple scoops.

Rollie pulled the gray up, looking back in the direction from which he had just traveled. Could Mort's claim be the motive behind the killings? Not likely. Why not just kill Mort and file on his claim. Rollie had seen it done. Sometimes nobody even paid any mind. Mostly folks figured if you couldn't hold onto what you had, you didn't deserve it.

Pursing his lips, the sheriff thought it over. Anything was possible, but Rollie couldn't see the sense in killing off half the country over a gold claim. And what about the mill? How did that fit into things?

Leaning forward in the saddle, Rollie patted the gray on the neck. "You know boy, there's a lot more going on here than meets the eye," he said out loud.

The gray shook his head, rattling the bit. The big horse tugged at the bit eager to be going. Laughing at the horse's eagerness, Rollie gave the gray his head.

Hank Bickerstaff waited at the edge of town, as Rollie rode in. The big rancher stood, hand on hips, his jaws working feverishly on a big wad of tobacco.

"Where the heck have you been? I've been looking for you all morning," Bickerstaff growled.

Rollie stared down from his horse, eyeing the big rancher with curious eyes. Obviously, Bickerstaff had something on his mind. "I've been out doing my sworn duty," Rollie replied tiredly. "What did you want to see me about?"

"One of my men was killed last night," Bickerstaff said flatly. He crossed his arms across his chest, staring a challenge at the sheriff. "Just what are you going to do about it?"

"Where did this happen?" Rollie asked, ignoring Bickerstaff's surliness.

"Not more than four miles from my ranch, by God!" Bickerstaff roared.

"How was the man killed?"

"He was shot in the back!" Bickerstaff shouted. "Now, are you going to arrest that tinhorn, Tinsworth?"

"What for?" Rollie asked mildly.

"What for!" Bickerstaff's normally florid face turned a dark red and spit flew from his lips as he sputtered. "That four flusher's been trying to take over the whole country."

"Funny, I heard the same thing about you," Rollie said mildly.

Bickerstaff wiped his mouth with the back of his hand, and pointed the hand directly at Rollie. "I'm serving notice. You either put a stop to that tinhorn, or I'll do it myself!"

Rollie's face hardened, his jaw jutting out stubbornly. "You just haul back on the reins, and simmer down. If somebody needs to be arrested, I'll do it. You try and interfere and I'll put you behind bars."

Bickerstaff placed his hands on his hips, his bull head forward. "What about my man who was killed? What do you plan on doing about that?" he asked his tone belligerent.

"I'll look into it," the sheriff promised. "When I know who done it, I'll arrest that man."

"You better be quick about it, my crew is mad. Harley wasn't a fighter, and he was well liked. They want somebody's head and they want it now."

"You keep your men under control," Rollie warned.

Rollie turned and stalked away, before the big rancher could reply. Walking up the street, Rollie felt at a loss. Having little experience in such matters, he didn't know what to do next.

As he walked by the hotel, he saw Sarah Eckles, Rebecca Moreland and Charles Tinsworth huddled in deep conversation.

Rollie stopped in the middle of the street, staring through the front window of the hotel. The three stood grouped around the counter and appeared to be having a very serious discussion.

"Now, I wonder what in blazes that's all about?" Rollie muttered, stepping up to the window for a closer look.

As he stepped to the window, Sarah Eckles looked up, her eyes meeting Rollie's. Hastily, she looked away, saying something to her companions.

Both Tinsworth and Rebecca Moreland turned to look out the window. Rebecca gave Rollie a cool measuring look, then turned and went upstairs.

For a second, Tinsworth's eyes met Rollie's. They stood locked in a stare, then Tinsworth smiled tauntingly and tipped his hat. With a last word to Sarah, the banker followed Rebecca up the stairs.

Rubbing his chin, Rollie backed away from the window. Two buildings down the street, he stopped, looking back at the hotel. Something about that little confab bothered him.

Being young ladies, it would be natural for Sarah Eckles and Rebecca Moreland to meet and talk but what would they have to discuss with Tinsworth?

Sarah had indicated that she didn't care for Tinsworth, and Rebecca didn't seem the type to waste time with a lot of empty chatter. Miss Rebecca Moreland struck Rollie as a serious down to business young woman. Surely not the type to engage in a lot of idle chit chat. Rollie would bet that woman didn't turn a tap unless she figured to get something out of it.

Scratching his jaw, Rollie slowly continued down the street. He might be doing Miss Moreland a disservice. She might not be at all what she seemed. Rollie reminded himself of that, but he didn't believe it. Not for a second. That was a hard young woman.

Maybe a talk with Ivan Moser would clear things up a bit. Rollie would bet that not much went on around this town without Moser knowing about it.

Moser looked up from the pot he was scrubbing, as Rollie entered the café. Smiling broadly, Moser dropped the pot back in the soapy water.

Ignoring the suds which splashed on his face, Moser headed for the stove and the coffee pot. He jerked his head toward the sink. "Better let that soak awhile," Moser said with a knowing smile.

Rollie tossed his hat on a table and pulled back a chair. As Rollie dropped into the chair, Moser sat a cup in front of him. "What can I do for ya? You want something to eat?"

Rollie shook his head, "I was wanting to ask you some questions," he said, watching as Moser filled the cup.

Moser filled his own cup and set the coffee pot in the middle of the table. "Ask away. I got plenty of answers. Wrong answers are free. Good ones cost some," Moser replied cheerfully as he eased his bulk into a chair.

Rollie smiled, shaking his head. Dang it, he liked this man. "I've been thinking about these killings. Since I can't go to the spot and track the killer back to his house, I figured to come at things from a different angle."

Rollie paused, tasting his coffee. Moser leaned forward, an eager expression on his face. "Sounds like a good way to go. What were you thinking?"

"I thought if I knew something about the men who were killed, maybe I could figure out why they were killed. If I knew why, figuring out who done it might be easy."

Moser blew out a big sigh, leaning back in his chair. "That's just the deal, there doesn't seem to be any rhyme or reason to these killings."

Moser drained his coffee cup and leaned forward for the pot. He dragged the pot across the table and started to fill his cup. He lifted the pot above the cup, then stopped.

"When old Jim Killigan turned up dead, most folks reckoned that either Bickerstaff or Tinsworth done it. Jim had the best ranch in these parts and you can bet both Hank and Tinsworth been looking at it and licking their chops. Naturally, folks assumed he was killed for that."

Moser filled his cup, looking across the table, holding the pot out. Rollie glanced in his cup and saw it was still almost full. Shaking his head, Rollie waited for the old cook to continue.

"Then when the sheriff was killed, most folks figured that he musta learned who the killer was."

"That makes sense, I reckon," Rollie agreed. "What about the rest of the men that were killed?"

Moser ran a red hand across his forehead and laughed without humor. "That's the rub. The rest of the men that were killed were just drifters or cowhands. No reason for anyone to want them dead. Except for maybe Ben Riggs."

Moser stopped; he looked at the ceiling and rubbed his brow again. "Ben took care of the jail; maybe the killer thought the sheriff told Ben something."

"Ben Riggs have any enemies?"

"Naw, Moser replied, quickly. "Everybody liked ol' Ben. There was even talk of making him mayor." Moser leaned back. "I really don't have time to do the job proper, and Ben woulda been a good man for the job. Can't think why anybody would wish harm on him."

"I was just thinking, those other men were all shot and Ben was killed with a knife. Maybe someone in town held a grudge against Ben and they done him in, figuring it would be blamed on whoever killed those other men."

"Could be, I suppose," Moser admitted with a shrug. "But I don't hardly think so. I mean sure, those other men were all shot, but they were killed a long ways from town, too. If a body was to shoot a gun in town, he would be up to his neck in town folk before he could hardly turn around. Doing it quiet like with a knife only makes sense."

What Moser said was sure enough true, but Rollie was remembering the moccasin track he found. The sheriff hadn't mentioned anything about moccasin tracks in his notebook. Somehow, Ben Riggs' murder seemed different than the others.

Rollie sipped his coffee, looking quietly across the table at Moser. "Some folks think that Bickerstaff is behind the killings," Rollie suggested, casually.

Moser frowned, staring intently into his cup. "I never thought so. Hank is a hard man and rougher than a cob, but this don't seem like his style. Hank's pretty high handed in his dealings, but mostly he does things plain and out in the open."

Moser swirled his coffee, thinking it over. He pointed across the table at Rollie. "Don't think for a second that because Hank has a bunkhouse full of gun hands, that he can't take care of business his self." Moser rested his forearms on the table, pushing his cup to the center of the table. "I reckon if Hank took the notion that he wanted somebody dead, then he'd shoot the man down in the middle of the street. And that would be that."

Rollie nodded, slowly. That followed closely with his own opinion of Bickerstaff.

Moser stuck his finger in his cup, stirring the coffee slowly. "That Tinsworth, he's a critter of another breed," he said slowly. "I'd say that shooting a man in the back would be right up his alley. And he's got men working for him that would do it, too. You met Carney, and he ain't near the worst of them."

"I sent him packing," Rollie said, feeling some satisfaction.

"We heard," Moser said, grinning. "Bud Swenson came in town last night. He couldn't stop talking about it." Moser patted Rollie's shoulder with a paw-like hand. "You sure made a friend there."

"What about Sarah Eckles? What's her story?" Rollie asked, looking at the scarred table top and trying to sound casual.

"She came into town bout a year back. She bought the hotel and then she went to work. Ain't stopped working neither. That girl is gonna make something out of herself."

"She and Tinsworth friendly?"

Moser laughed dryly. "Not so's you would notice. I reckon Sarah has more brains than to tie up with a skunk like Tinsworth."

Moser looked up suddenly, a smile spreading across his face. "Say, you ain't getting a case on her, are you?"

Despite himself, Rollie felt his face burn and turn red. "No, I'm just trying to get folks placed, that's all."

"Sure, sure," Moser agreed instantly. He winked at Rollie. "Being sheriff and all, it's important to know who folks are. But you could do worse. Sarah's a right fine girl; like I said, a worker. She'll make someone a good wife."

Moser leaned half way across the table, his eyes shining bright. "If you was to settle here, I figure we could make a pile of money. There's plenty of opportunities for a couple of enterprising men like us."

"I heard about the flour mill."

Moser grinned slyly. "Heard about that? Figured you would, sooner or later." Moser hitched his chair closer. "See that mill is what really makes the freight business good. Killigan was gonna pay us to haul flour to Santa Fe, then we'd bring goods back."

"Make money coming and going?"

Moser licked his lips, rubbing his hands together. "You know it."

"You think the mill will ever get going now that Killigan is dead?"

"No reason why it shouldn't. It was a dang good idea, no matter who came up with it." A worried frown knitted up Moser's face. "I tried talking to that niece. You know, see if we could work something out, but I swear, talking to that gal is like bear hugging a cactus."

Rollie smiled, almost feeling sorry for Rebecca Moreland. Moser wasn't an easy man to say no to and he didn't give up easy. "You keep after her; I gotta ride out to Bickerstaff's."

"Yeah, I heard one of his fellas got killed. You be careful. I don't want to lose a partner."

"Don't worry, I'll be back."

Rollie rode from the town, stopping to roll a smoke and look back. From a distance, Cordova seemed like a peaceful place. No one could guess that there had been several killings. And there would be more, unless Rollie could stop it.

His mood broken, Rollie tossed away the cigarette and pointed the gray in the direction of Hank Bickerstaff's ranch. Rollie settled comfortably in the saddle, letting the gray pick his own gate.

The sun was high in the sky when Rollie crossed onto Bickerstaff's range. Before long, Rollie began to see cattle marked with Bickerstaff's slash B brand.

Curious, Rollie kneed the gray over and rode through the herd. Right away, Rollie could see that whatever else he might be, Bickerstaff was a first rate cattleman. The animals were in good shape, the early morning's sun shining on their glossy coats. Soon, Bickerstaff would have to make a drive since most of the cattle were ready for market.

Leaving the cattle behind, Rollie rode over to where Bickerstaff's man had been killed. As expected, the tracks had been trampled, so Rollie dismounted and climbed up to the spot where the shot came from.

There he learned two things. The killer was the same man that killed Jim Killigan. Judging from the way the man choose his ambush spot, the way he fired one shot and then slipped away, Rollie felt sure it was the same man. The man was supremely confident in his ability. He fired one shot from a very long range. The killer hadn't gone down to his victim to make sure, he simply fired the one shot then rode away.

Rollie leaned against a boulder and took off his hat. Wiping the sweat from his face, Rollie bleakly looked up at the sun. A man that sure of his abilities surely had to have done this very thing before, probably lots of times. A professional.

Mounting the gray, Rollie began to back track the shooter. At first, the tracking was easy, as Bickerstaff's men had trailed him and their tracks were plain to see. For a couple of miles, Rollie followed the trail at a lope. Occasionally, he stopped and made sure Bickerstaff's men hadn't lost the trail, but he could always find the tracks of the killer's horse mixed in with those of Bickerstaff's riders.

After almost four miles, the trail ended abruptly. Rollie could plainly see where Bickerstaff's men had stopped. The way their horses had shifted around indicated a long meeting. Then in a tight bunch, they had cut for town.

Turning the gray loose to graze, Rollie began to cast about for the lost trail on foot. Working in ever widening circles, Rollie poured over the ground looking for any kind of sign. Bickerstaff's men hadn't found the trail and neither did Rollie. It simply vanished. Whoever killed that man, knew how to cover his tracks and he had chosen this spot to lose any pursuers.

Squatting on his heels, Rollie rolled a smoke and studied the country. If the killer had picked this spot to lose his followers, that likely meant that he was going to change directions, but which way? Had he turned left or right or doubled back completely?

No way of knowing. Or was there? A wave of excitement coming over him, Rollie trotted to the gray and took the sheriff's day book from the saddlebag. Opening the book, Rollie reviewed the locations of where every man had been killed and the direction the killer had taken afterwards.

Using a stick, Rollie drew a rough map of the country in the dirt, marked the spot of the killings, and then drew a line representing the direction the killer had taken.

In each case, the killer had headed roughly in the direction of Mort's claim. Rollie didn't think for a second that the old prospector was behind the killings, but his claim seemed to be the central location.

Curious, Rollie stuffed the daybook back into his saddlebag, then mounted the gray. He urged the big horse into a lope and pointed him straight in the direction of Mort's claim.

As he rode, Rollie remained alert for any tracks. Whatever the killer had done to hide his trail would be bothersome and he wouldn't keep it up forever.

Midafternoon, he stopped to give the gray a drink and a rest. He hadn't packed any grub for himself, so Rollie had to be content to listen to his belly rumble as the gray tugged at the tough grass.

After an hour, Rollie continued on his way. Riding along, Rollie noticed a curious low mound off to the south. Reining his horse in, Rollie stood in the stirrups, studying the mound. Something about the rise bothered Rollie. It looked out of place.

Pushing the mound from his mind, Rollie touched a spur to the gray. The big horse barely took two steps before Rollie hauled back savagely on the reins. Startled and upset, the gray reared and danced sideways. Fighting for control, Rollie managed to keep his seat until the gray settled down.

Dropping the reigns, Rollie sprang from the saddle. Snorting angrily, the big horse shied away a few steps. Ignoring the antics of the horse, Rollie knelt down to examine the ground.

"I knew it!" he said, smacking his fist into his palm as he stared at the perfect track on the ground.

The track was the same horse the killer rode!

Whistling for the gray to follow, Rollie duck-walked forward looking for the next track. What he found was a rock torn loose from its resting spot.

Forgetting about the heat and his hunger, Rollie became engrossed in the task of working out the trail. Tirelessly, he dog-trotted back and forth seeking the next sign. By now, Rollie had the stride of the horse measured, giving him a good idea where to look for the next track. Still it was slow going.

The unknown rider had kept his speed down, making Rollie's task more difficult, but the sheriff stuck with the job. Sweat rolled down his back, soaking his shirt, but Rollie paid little attention to that. His mind was consumed with the trail. At times he wouldn't see a track for several yards and he had to follow more by feel than anything else.

Abruptly, the trail came to a small canyon, cutting across the prairie floor. After turning the gray loose to graze, Rollie cautiously approached the lip of the canyon.

The edge of the canyon dropped straight down ten feet. Below the drop-off was a narrow slide, then another drop. A small stream of water ran sluggishly along the bottom of the canyon.

Down the canyon a hundred yards or so was a cut in the wall. A good place to get down to the bottom, Rollie figured. More than likely the place the unknown rider used. In either direction as far as Rollie could see that was the only place a rider was going to cross this canyon.

Rollie straightened slowly; hopefully, he might pick up the trail on that slope. By now the killer would be sure he had lost his pursuers and might be more careless. Rollie hoped so, but he didn't really count on it. He had the feeling that being careful was a part of this gent's nature.

As he turned to fetch the gray horse, Rollie heard a shot and felt a hot flash of pain in his chest. Rollie cried out and instinctively took a step back. For a second he hung on the lip of the canyon, fighting for balance. Waving his arms he toppled over.

He hit the first slope with a jolt that almost paralyzed him. His body sliding down the slope, Rollie flopped over the second, landing flat on his back in the bottom of the canyon.

Half dazed, his arm in the water, Rollie tried to get up and found he couldn't move. As he tried to draw some air into his pain-racked lungs, Rollie saw the shadow of a man. The killer was coming to finish the job!

CHAPTER FIVE

Blood ran in Rollie's eyes and his chest felt as if it were on fire. Rollie wasn't sure if he was hurt bad. He didn't feel bad hurt, but just raising his arm to wipe the blood from his eyes was enough to send a bolt of pain shooting through him. One thing he knew hurt or not, if he did not move, he was a dead man.

Ignoring the flash of pain, Rollie hitched his body over next to the canyon wall. Sucking back against the wall, Rollie realized he didn't have his rifle. Glancing about frantically, he saw the weapon lying at the edge of the water, a good ten feet away. Rollie started to move to retrieve the rifle, when he heard a sound from up top. Looking longingly at the rifle, Rollie pulled one of his pistols and hugged back against the wall of the canyon.

Rollie heard a grunt and rocks cascaded over the ledge as the killer jumped down to the small slope. Moving only his head, Rollie glanced up. As he watched, the barrel of a rifle slowly appeared when the killer leaned out for a better look. Lunging up, Rollie grabbed the rifle barrel and jerked down hard. With a cry, the man sailed over Rollie's head and landed flat on his back into the water.

Abandoning the captured rifle, Rollie waded in after him. Clenching his teeth against the pain in his chest, Rollie floundered in the knee deep water. Grabbing a handful of matted hair, Rollie jerked the man's head from the water, sending a roundhouse punch crashing into the man's face. That one felt pretty good so Rollie splattered him again.

Towing the man by the hair, Rollie drug the killer back to the shore. Rollie pushed the man and laughed as the man slammed into the wall then bounced back, flopping down into the sand.

Rollie wiped the blood and water from his face, then stooped over and retrieved his own rifle. He swore looking at the rifle. The stock was a ruined mess of splinters. Rollie looked down at his side and discovered several splinters stuck in his side. One the size of a pencil. Grimacing in pain, Rollie pulled the splinters from his side.

Rollie tucked his own rifle under his arm and retrieved the rifle the killer had dropped. Carefully, he wiped the sand from the action and made certain the barrel was clear.

Pointing the rifle one-handed, Rollie slowly approached his prisoner. The man was groaning and starting to show some signs of life when Rollie rolled him over. For a long second, Rollie stared at his prisoner, not believing what he saw.

"Claude Baines!" he whispered.

Baines mistook Rollie's exclamation for a question and he wasn't in no mood to answer anything. He coughed a couple of times and worked his jaw back and forth. "What do you want?" he finally asked, still rubbing the spot on his jaw where Rollie hit him.

Rollie glared down at the fallen man. Baines didn't recognize him. "All I want is you on your feet, for now," Rollie growled, punctuating the order by jabbing Baines in the ribs with his rifle.

His expression surly, Baines climbed slowly to his feet. His lips set in a thin line, Baines glared defiantly at Rollie. "You gonna kill me, now?"

"Lord knows I ought to," Rollie muttered, liking the notion. Baines' face went white as Rollie trained the rifle on him. Baines staggered back a few steps. "Hey, now," he said putting his palms out. "You don't want to pull that trigger."

"Sure I do," Rollie grunted, taking a better grip on the rifle. Rollie had chased this man for years, but now after all this time, Rollie couldn't bring himself to pull the trigger. "Aw crud," Rollie sighed, lowering his rifle slightly.

Baines laughed, a sneer springing to his lips. "You ain't got the guts," he accused. "You might as well let me go. You ain't got the guts to kill me."

"What I'm gonna do is arrest you and if you say one word before we get to town, I'll bend this rifle over your noggin."

Holding his ribs with one hand, Rollie stayed behind Baines as they climbed out of the canyon. "Stop right there," Rollie ordered as they emerged back out on the prairie. Rollie whistled sharply and the gray came trotting up, stirrups flapping. Rollie took his rope off the saddle and shook out a loop. Grinning wickedly at Baines, Rollie dropped the loop around the outlaw's neck. "Let's go get your horse," Rollie grunted.

Baines cursed under his breath. "I ain't helping you."

"Suit yourself," Rollie said cheerfully. "It's a far piece into town; take us a while with you walking." Rollie grinned at Baines, enjoying himself. "We got time. Course if it gets late, you can always run."

Baines swore bitterly. He folded his arms across his chest. Laughing, Rollie swung aboard the gray. "Alright let's go."

Baines kicked the dirt, and then jerked his head to the east. "He's over there," he muttered through clenched teeth.

"Good enough, lead the way." Baines led the way to a small group of rocks where a bay horse was tied. "Nice horse," Rollie commented and gave the rope a healthy jerk for good measure. "Get aboard. I'll let you ride him one last time before we hang you," Rollie instructed, waiting patiently for Baines to mount. Rollie smiled at Baines as he tied the rope around his saddle horn. "You try anything and I'll jerk you outta the saddle and drag you to town."

Rollie's threat must have impressed Baines, because Claude hardly moved or spoke a word during the long trip back to town, which suited Rollie to a tee. All the way to town Rollie worried about what he would do with Baines. It was clear Baines didn't recognize him; Rollie had changed a lot in ten years. Baines didn't recognize him now, but he would know the name. Rollie did not want that. He should just kill Baines and be done with it.

Rollie was still thinking about it when he came to the fork in the trail. Down the left fork he could see Marge Ross' place.

Somehow the place reminded Rollie of Marge herself. Broad and sprawling, but bustling with energy. Even in the fading light, Rollie could see pigs milling about in a pen, and chickens pecking in the yard. Dangling from a clothesline, laundry fluttered in the breeze.

As Rollie watched, a man came out of the house, stopping short when he saw Rollie. Rollie raised a hand, but the man just hurried to a horse tied by the barn.

Rollie chuckled, continuing on his way. Looked like Burke, the storekeeper. Rollie hadn't heard that Burke delivered supplies but that wouldn't cut no ice with Marge Ross. Rollie would bet if Marge said deliver, then Burke would scorch the ground getting them out there.

Rollie chuckled again at the very thought of the wormy, little Burke bucking up and telling Marge he wouldn't deliver. She'd wring his scrawny neck.

"I wouldn't be laughing now," Baines said, speaking for the first time since they started to town. "My friends will come to get me. You'll be lucky to still be breathing by morning."

"Shut up or I swear, I'll kill you now and be done with it."

"Hah," Baines said with a laugh. "You couldn't kill me before, you ain't gonna do it now."

"No?" Rollie grunted. "I might not kill you, but I sure might slap you outta the saddle and drag you to town."

"You ain't got the guts. You never did have. I seen that way back when, out at Joe Turner's place."

"You recognized me?"

Baines nodded. "Took me a while, but I figured it out." Baines sneered at Rollie. "Heard you been looking for me all these years."

Rollie didn't answer, feeling a dreadful shame wash over him. Baines laughed a snarling sound. "Must be something to chase after someone all these years, then not have the guts to pull the trigger."

"Well if you're so tough and you knew I was chasing you why didn't you let me catch up?" Rollie taunted.

Baines shrugged. "Cause I knew it didn't matter. I knew you was too yellow to do it."

"Good thing that it doesn't matter," Rollie said. "You took a shot at a sheriff. The town will hang you for that."

"Don't bet on it. I figure to be a free man by morning."

"You seem mighty sure. You ain't been there long. Bickerstaff might not want to bother with busting you out."

Baines smiled, but Rollie imagined that he could see a nugget of worry underneath the smile. "We'll see." With that Baines fell silent, which suited Rollie just fine. Now that Baines had recognized him, Rollie had to worry about what the town would think when they found out the truth.

Cordova came into sight and Rollie was still worrying over it. He sure hadn't come up with any ideas. Maybe he should just throw Baines in jail and deal with the truth later. Might be nice to get it out in the open and be done with it.

Ivan Moser stood at the window of his café, watching the street as Rollie rode into town. A frown crossed the cook's beefy face as he recognized the sheriff's prisoner. With a quick jerk, Ivan tore off his apron and tossed it on the counter. "I gotta go talk to the sheriff. I'll be back in a minute," he called to his wife.

"Ivan Moser, don't you go running off! The supper crowd will be coming in soon," Ethel Moser shouted as she came out of the kitchen, only to see the door closing behind her husband. She stomped the floor with her foot and placed her hands on her hips and glared at the door.

By the time Moser reached the jail, he had a full head of steam and burst through the door with all the stealth of a tornado. He skidded to a halt, placing his hands on his hips as he glared at the new sheriff. "Look, Dukes, I didn't hire you to go out and settle personal scores. You were supposed to be tracking down a killer!"

Rollie finished locking the cell door behind Baines. He checked the lock then tossed the keys on the desk. "I didn't know you hired me. I thought it was the town," Rollie countered, flopping tiredly into his chair.

A little more color shot to Moser's ruddy face, but it didn't slow him down any. "Yeah? Well, I'm the one that backed you for this job. That makes me sorta responsible," Moser bellered. "I assured folks that you could do the job. What am I supposed to tell them now?"

Before Rollie could even think about answering, the door flew open, banging against the wall. Her eyes blazing, Rebecca Moreland stormed in like a blizzard sweeping across the plains. She shoved Moser aside and marched right up to the desk. "Sheriff Dukes, I must protest your actions! Why aren't you trying to find my uncles murderer? What kind of lawman do you call yourself?" she demanded, stomping her foot against the floor.

"That's just what I was doing. I was tracking the killer when Baines took a shot at me," Rollie explained, maybe stretching the truth a mite. Feeling exhausted, he rubbed his aching forehead. "Now, if you two would clear out, I'd like to go over to the hotel and get some sleep."

Both Rebecca Moreland and Ivan Moser had different ideas. Neither had spoken their piece yet and they didn't intend to leave until they got it off their chests. Of the two, Rebecca acted the quickest, jabbing a finger at him. "I understand that you have had personal difficulties with this man, but now is not the time for you to be settling private grudges," Rebecca said with the tone of a parent scolding a child. "What you should be doing is concentrating on finding the man that killed my uncle and the others.

Despite the weariness weighing him down, Rollie felt his temper flare. Usually, he tried to keep his temper under control, but tonight he didn't even bother. He half rose out of his chair, pointing a finger across the desk, stabbing it at Miss Moreland. "Look lady, I was out on the trail before sun up, I been shot, slid down a mountain, fell off a cliff and right now I'm in no mood to hear your complaints."

One look was enough to tell him that Rebecca was not impressed. Her face turned sour as she crossed her arms over her chest. She flipped a hand at him, as if brushing away his excuses. "I do believe that is your job. That is what the town is paying you for. If you ask me, it's time for you to produce results instead of flimsy excuses."

Moser, who had been strangely quiet, now stepped forward, his eyes on the floor. He jammed his hands down in his pockets and cleared his throat, shifting his weight from foot to foot. Whatever he was going to say was cut off by the crash of breaking glass.

A rock the size of a man's fist crashed through the window, spraying glass across the desk. Even before the rock quit rolling, Rollie sprang to his feet and crossed to the window in three long bounds.

His hand falling to his gun, Rollie looked out the window and what he saw twisted his guts into a knot and made his blood run cold.

CHAPTER SIX

Rollie spun away from the window and in three quick bounds crossed to the row of guns.

Running a quick eye over the weapons, he snatched a short, wicked-looking shotgun off the rack. He broke the weapon open, checking to make sure both barrels were loaded. Assured that the gun was ready to fire, Rollie snapped it closed and looked at his two guests. "You might want to find some cover. This is gonna get ugly."

With that said, Rollie stepped out the door, running silently around the building in his socks. Rounding the corner he burst into the alley. Holding the shotgun casually, his eyes traveling over the mob in front of him. Not much of a mob. Only six men. "You boys are out kinda late." Rollie looked at their leader. "You'd be Lang. Anything I can do for you?" Rollie asked, holding the shotgun loosely in his hands.

Lang stood in the front of the group, holding a torch. Obviously their leader, he took a step forward. "We came to get Claude Baines," he said, his tone confident. Lang was a short, stocky man in his late forties. A hard man, he took a step forward, ready to fight. "Claude is a friend of mine."

Rollie pushed his hat back, smiling innocently at Lang. "I'm sorry to disappoint you, but Baines is under arrest. He's going to stay right where he is until his trial."

A roar went up from the mob, which Lang silenced with a sweep of his hand. He turned back to Rollie, his face hard. "You got no call to arrest Baines. He wasn't even in the country when most of them fellers got themselves kilt."

Normally, Rollie might have tried to reason with the mob, but tonight he was in no mood. He was bone tired, and just got his butt royally chewed twice in less than five minutes. His ribs were aching and he was scraped and bruised from head to toe. All and all, Rollie Dukes was in a miserable mood.

So, instead of trying to appease the crowd, he took a quick step forward and drove the butt of the shotgun into Lang's belly. As Lang melted to the ground, Rollie reversed the shotgun and directed it at the crowd.

"Now, I appreciate you boys taking a civic interest in the running of this town, but I'm the sheriff and when I need your advice, I'll come ask for it," Rollie drawled casually. He straightened up and all signs of friendliness left his voice. "Now, I suggest you go back about your business before I lock the lot of you up."

With their leader doubled over at their feet, the mob lost a little of their starch. The men in the front gazed upon the unblinking eye of the shotgun and realized there were other places they'd rather be. Almost as one they eased back a step. Rollie smiled a wicked grin at them. He knew, right about then, each of them was wondering why they were here.

They were ready to run and before they had a chance to screw their nerve back up, a rifle barrel poked through the window of the jail, shattering the glass. Rollie didn't bother to turn and look; instead, he smiled at the crowd and repeated the order for them to move out.

These boys hadn't thought things out before they'd come marching over to free their comrade, but you can believe, they were doing a pile of calculations right about then. They began to take note of the fact that they were standing, packed in that alley. If a ruckus started, a bunch of them weren't going to make it. That shotgun was gonna take out at least two of them. Almost as one, they began to shuffle away.

"Drag him along with you," Rollie instructed, pointing to Lang. He watched as two men helped Lang to his feet and dragged him over to the saloon. As the last of the men disappeared into the saloon, Rollie turned back to the jail.

"Thanks for the help," he said to Moser, who was still holding the rifle and peering out the broken window.

"Looked like you could use a hand," Moser replied quietly. He looked at the rifle with the ruined stock. "Glad I didn't have to use this. Wasn't even sure if it would shoot." He grinned ruefully and scratched his ample stomach. "Sorry about crawling you earlier. I reckon this whole mess has got under my skin." Moser tossed the rifle back on the desk, then looked gravely at Rollie. The cook mopped a bit of sweat off his brow. "You gotta find this killer. The lid's about ready to blow off this whole country."

"I know," Rollie growled in frustration. "I'm doing the best I can. There just isn't a lot to go on."

"Quite obviously, your best just isn't good enough," Rebecca said tightly. She crossed her arms and tapped her foot on the floor. "Just when do you plan to catch my uncle's killer?"

"I don't know ma'am," Rollie replied tiredly. "Like I said, I'm doing everything I can. One thing is sure, I ain't gonna catch him standing here jawing with you."

Rebecca's lips compressed down into flat lines as she stabbed her finger at Rollie. "Then I suggest you go out and start doing your job," she snapped. Spinning on her heel, she stomped out of the office.

"I'm afraid you're gonna have trouble with that young lady," Moser said with a chuckle, a small laugh that carried precious little humor. "She's been talking all over town. Stirring folks up. She sure didn't care for the fact that you told her she had to wait to take over her uncle's ranch." Moser chuckled dryly. "That's a young lady with money on her mind."

"I thought you were gonna take care of that. I thought you were gonna show her all the money to be made if she goes ahead with the flour mill?" Rollie asked.

A hound dog expression riding sourly on his face, Moser shrugged heavily. "She don't want to hear nothing bout that. Guess we are too low class for her."

"I'm too tired to worry about that right now," Rollie replied with a groan. "All I want now is some sleep."

"You want me to watch the jail in case them fellers come back?" Moser offered.

"Naw. I don't think they will be back. To tell the truth, right now I don't even care," Rollie replied, yawning mightily.

"Suit yourself," Moser said with a nod. He tossed the rifle on the desk and lumbered over to the door. "You need anything, just let me know."

"Yeah sure," Rollie replied, waving absently as Moser disappeared out the door and into the night. Wearily, Rollie heaved himself out of his chair. He picked up his rifle. The stock was ruined. He'd have to carve a new one. Rollie glanced at the rack, thinking there might be a rifle he could use until his was fixed. The rack was a big disappointment. Besides the shotgun Rollie had used, there was an old muzzle loader and another shotgun. Rollie glanced at Baines' rifle. Somehow, he didn't want to use it. He had money; maybe he should buy a new one.

He could stop by the store in the morning.

With that Rollie grabbed his hat, and bent to get his boots. As he scooped up his boots, Rollie froze in his tracks.

For a fleeting second, something flashed in his mind, then it was gone. The hair on the back of his neck standing up, Rollie stared thoughtfully at his boots. He had an uneasy feeling, like somebody just stepped on his grave. It was like when you heard a sound in the night, but couldn't see anything there.

Rollie dropped back into his chair and concentrated on what he'd just missed, but nothing leapt to his tired mind. Still as he tugged his boots on, he couldn't shake the feeling that he'd missed something. Something deadly.

The doubt still nagging at his mind, Rollie trudged over to his room. Hoping Burke had come back and opened the store, Rollie swung by, thinking he would feel better once he replaced his rifle.

The door to the store was locked and the inside dark. Dang Burke should be back, unless he stayed out at Marge's for supper, which Rollie couldn't even imagine. Feeling uncomfortable without a rifle, Rollie drug his feet over to his room.

Despite the fact that he was bone tired, Rollie didn't sleep well. His side was aching, making it hard to get comfortable.

He was tossing and turning, punching his pillow into shape when it came to him. What he had missed earlier.

How had Bickerstaff's men gotten into town so fast.

Seemed like Rollie had barely gotten Baines in the jail before Lang and his men showed up. Closing his eyes Rollie thought back.

It surely hadn't been much over an hour after locking Baines up before Bickerstaff's men came up the alley.

How had they even known?

Rollie was still puzzling over it when he heard it. The solitary creak of a floorboard. Instantly wide awake, Rollie froze in place, his ears straining. He listened quietly for a long moment, but could catch no other sound.

Rollie knew, if someone had been walking down the hall normally, he would have heard something else. Another protest from the board as the weight came off it, a next footstep, something. But there was nothing.

The fact that no other sound came from the hallway told Rollie one thing. Somebody had been creeping down the hall, and now, they had frozen in place, lurking outside his door. Question was; what would they do now?

Really, the creeper had only two choices. Wait a few seconds and gently try to creep forward, or move quickly, coming through the door in a rush. Coming in a rush would be the most effective, but that took a lot of gumption, most folks wouldn't have it in them. Course the jasper that had been doing all the killing, he surely wasn't most folks. He had more than his share of gumption.

Rollie felt an icy finger run down his back. He flicked a quick glance to his gun belt, holding the two Smiths. It hung from the bedpost a scant few feet from him. Rollie knew if that door crashed open now, those pistols might as well be on the moon. There just wasn't anyway he would get to them in time. The creeper could fire several times before Rollie could snatch one of them.

He needed one of them pistols in his hands.

Trying to shift his weight without making the bed squeak, Rollie twisted his body towards the guns, reaching out slowly. As he reached for the guns, Rollie kept his eyes glued to the doorknob. If it moved, he would roll out of bed, hopefully snagging one of the pistols in the process.

When his hand closed over the smooth grip of the pistol, Rollie felt much better. At least now, he had a fighting chance. He eased the pistol free from the holster, but didn't cock it. Rollie had no intention of making the same mistake as the creeper. He knew he couldn't get off the bed without making any noise, so he wasn't even going to try.

Sucking in a deep breath, Rollie launched himself off the bed, crossing the room in a single bound, jerking the door open. He caught a quick glimpse of a dark figure in the hallway, then crashed into the man, driving him across the hallway and into the far wall. Rollie grabbed an arm, slinging the man through the open door and into the room. Pinning the man against the wall, Rollie kicked the door shut. That was about the time when he became well aware of the fact that it wasn't a man that he was pushing around.

Rollie stepped back quickly, leveling his gun at Rebecca Moreland. "Mind telling me why you are sneaking around outside my door?"

"I wanted to talk to you, but I didn't want anyone to know about it."

"Why? Why would you care? You sure didn't care who saw when you were chewing me out earlier."

Rebecca lowered her head, batting her eyes at him. "Sorry about that. I didn't realize what was going on here."

Rollie raised an eyebrow. "What is going on here?"

"Well, to begin with, Mister Tinsworth is trying to cheat me out of my uncle's ranch!"

Despite himself, Rollie was interested. "How do you mean?"

Rebecca inched closer to Rollie, her hip almost touching his leg. "He has some paper. He claims my uncle signed, borrowing a lot of money. He says if I don't pay it back, he will take my uncle's ranch. Can he do that?"

"Maybe. I don't know."

"I thought you were the sheriff. Shouldn't you know about such things?"

"Probably," Rollie admitted. "I'm not a real lawman. They just hired me to deal with this mess. I don't know much about that other stuff"

She reached up, touching Rollie's shoulder lightly, letting her fingertips linger, then run down his arm. "But you could help me." She rubbed his hand, looking up with large brown eyes. "I mean if you wanted to, you could help me." She slid a half step closer, giving his arm a soft squeeze. "Don't you want to help me?"

She leaned in a little more. "You could stop him," she said and Rollie could feel her breath on his cheek. "You're not afraid of him, not like the others. Are you?"

"No. I am not!" Rollie said, having a little trouble with his breathing. He eased back a step, feeling hot all over. He wiped a little sweat from his brow.

"So you will help me?" she asked following him.

A part of Rollie was screaming not to trust her, but a big part of him was noticing how good she smelled. "You could help me, I mean if you really wanted too," she purred inching a bit closer. "It would mean a lot to me."

"I don't know what I could do," Rollie croaked, his throat suddenly dry.

"You could go out there with me tomorrow. Out to Uncle Jim's ranch. Let me take over. Tell Mister Tinsworth to back off. He would listen to you. I think he is afraid of you."

Rollie was ready to promise her the moon, when several shots rang out. The shots were a quick, ragged volley, then dead silence.

CHAPTER SEVEN

The sound of the shots echoed through the town, slapping off the buildings and fading away into the night, Moser and the storekeeper, Joshua Burke were the first ones out into the street. Moser wore only a long night shirt, hanging almost to his ankles. Burke wore dark pants and a striped shirt, but both of them carried rifles. Wearing confused looks, they waved their guns up and down the empty street.

Rollie burst into the street a few seconds later. "See anything?" he asked.

"No, dang it," Moser muttered, gripping his rifle and looking mad enough to bite the head off a buffalo. "Somebody's dead! You can bet your bottom dollar on that," he growled, saying what they were all thinking.

Looking like a giant red bear, shirtless and his suspenders flapping behind him, Hartshorn pounded around the corner, carrying a shotgun. "Nobody back here," he said, out of breath. "Shots sounded like they came from the jail," he added.

Rollie exchanged a quick look with Moser, and then sprang across the street towards the jail. Rollie was the first one there, beating the storekeeper Burke by a few steps. Grimacing at the acrid smell of spent gunpowder, Rollie pounded through the office and back to the jail. Two long steps into the jail, Rollie skidded to a stop, knowing there was no need to hurry.

Baines lay on his side in the bunk, one arm thrown wide. His head lolled off to one side, as if his neck had turned limber as a grass rope. Even before he saw the bullet holes stitching up Baines' back, Rollie knew the man was dead. There was a slackness to his body that Rollie recognized.

Burke, who had slammed into Rollie when the sheriff stopped, was now peering over Rollie's shoulder. The storekeeper swore, turning away as Moser and Hartshorn pounded into the jail, shaking the whole building.

Wheezing like a windstorm, Moser put his hands on his knees. "What happened?" he asked, between puffs.

"It's Baines," Rollie answered, turning away from the cell. "He's dead."

They all looked at Rollie, suspicion springing to their faces. "Hey, it wasn't me!" Rollie protested, spreading his hands.

The three men shared a look. Hartshorn turned slightly away with a shrug, but Burke nodded eagerly. "Alright," Moser sighed. "Guess we better see your guns, sheriff," Moser said, his voice stern as he held out a paw-like hand. "Pass 'em on over."

"I was in my hotel room, asleep," Rollie said, fudging the truth. For some reason he felt uncomfortable saying Rebecca Moreland had been in his room. His face burning a little red Rollie pulled his gun belt from his shoulder and passing it over to Moser. "Sarah saw me leave my room right after the shots. No way I coulda got back there so fast."

"Don't worry, we'll ask her," Moser grunted, pulling one of Rollie's pistols from its holster. He checked the cylinder making sure the weapon was loaded, and then handed it across to Hartshorn.

"Barrel's cold," Hartshorn said, as Moser checked the other pistol.

"If I was going to kill Baines, why would I drag him all the way to town? I coulda just killed him and hid the body and no one would have been the wiser," Rollie pointed out as Moser finished checking the guns.

"They haven't been fired," Moser decided, sighing heavily. "Sorry Rollie, my boy, but we had to be sure."

"Well, if he didn't kill him, who did?" Hartshorn wondered, as he passed Rollie's pistol back over.

"Sure doesn't make any sense. Who besides Rollie would want to kill Baines?" Burke asked.

"Well we know it wasn't Rollie. We all got out in the street together. Wasn't time for him to kill Baines and get out in the street when he did," Moser pointed out.

"Well, somebody sure as shootin' killed him. But who? He ain't hardly been here long enough to make enemies," Burke said, wiping his nose with the back of his hand. "If the sheriff didn't kill him, and I'm not so sure about that, who did?"

"Come on Burke," Moser urged, showing some exasperation. "Rollie got into the street right behind us and his guns ain't been fired tonight. I'd say we can be sure it wasn't him."

"Maybe, but there are a lot of guns in the sheriff's office. Maybe he used one of them." Burke said, glaring a challenge at Rollie.

"Sounds far-fetched," Hartshorn replied quietly.

Burke looked ready to argue, but instead shrugged. "Reckon you're right. I'm just kinda on edge" He wiped a hand across his mouth. "We gotta stop these killings."

"No argument there," Moser grunted.

"Well if Rollie didn't kill Baines. Who did? Why would anyone want to kill him?" Burke wondered, and then shook his head. He glanced over at Rollie. "You think he saw something out at Diablo Canyon?"

Rollie frowned, thinking that Burke was likely right. He nodded to the little storekeeper. "I reckon you are right. Everything seems to point out there. Maybe first thing in the morning, I should go back out there."

They all exchanged a quick look, but it was Burke who spoke up. "I don't know about that," he said slowly. "With everything that has happened, it might be best if you were in town."

"But the key to this whole thing is out there. I'm sure of it." Rollie protested.

"I was thinking about Bickerstaff," Burke replied. "Hank is a hard man and that crew of his is thugs at best. They might not look kindly that one of them was murdered in the jail. What if they come to town?"

Rollie shrugged, knowing they couldn't afford to just wait it out. Somehow they had to find out what was really going on. "What do you fellas think?" he asked, turning to Moser and Hartshorn.

It was Moser who replied, rubbing his jaw. "I don't know, Rollie." He glanced at Hartshorn, who only shrugged his heavy shoulders. Moser blew out a heavy sigh. "Alright, go do what you gotta do. I guess we can hold the lid on for one more day."

Rollie and Hartshorn carried the body the livery, laying Barnes out on a heavy table in the back. "You got to put a stop to this," he said. "I'm spending all my time building coffins."

"Yeah," Rollie grunted, his mind whirling as he wandered away.

Rollie tossed and turned, trying to sleep. The bed was soft as cat fur, but still sleep wouldn't come. Rollie punched the pillow, closing his eyes, trying to will himself to sleep. His brain wouldn't shut down. He'd missed something. He could feel it. A spooky feeling, like a fellow got sometimes out in the woods. Like somebody was watching him.

His mind kept circling the idea, like a vulture over a carcass. Something important had happened tonight. All of a sudden, Rollie sat straight up in bed, the cobwebs fleeing his mind.

Burke! What was it he said? Rollie absently scratched his chin, trying to remember exactly what had been said. Something important was lurking on the fringes of his mind. One of them had said there wasn't any reason for anyone other than Rollie to kill Baines, and then Burke had replied that it must have something to do with Diablo Canyon.

How did Burke know Baines had been at Diablo Canyon?

Rollie hadn't mentioned that, to anyone except Moser. So how did Burke know?

Because he was in on whatever was going on.

Excited, Rollie rolled out of bed, padding around his tiny room, feeling the rough boards of the floor through holes in his socks. Rollie stopped. His mind racing back. Burke had been at Marge Ross' place. Burke saw him with Claude Baines!

If Burke had ridden hard from Marge Ross' he coulda gotten to Bickerstaff's place about the time Rollie got into town.

Would there have been enough time for Bickerstaff's men to get into town?

Rollie had stabled the horses, spoke with Hartshorn some and then locked up Baines. He'd spoken with Moser and Rebecca. If they hustled, they might have had time.

Okay, he thought, now that I know Burke is my man, the rest should be easy. He just had to prove it.

Rollie wanted to talk to Moser. He respected the old cook's opinions, and the man knew everybody in this town. More than that, Moser knew everybody's business. Shooting a glance at the window, Rollie scowled at the darkness. It was still too early to catch Moser.

Muttering under his breath and smacking his fist into his palm, Rollie resumed his pacing. So, he knew Burke was involved. What else did he know? Burke had been one of the first ones in the street after Baines was gunned down in the jail. Maybe Burke didn't come from his house, but from the jail. That would explain how he got in the street so fast. Plus he was dressed!

None of the others were fully dressed, but Burke had been. Rollie closed his eyes picturing the street. It would have been easy for Burke to run behind the jail, cut between the buildings and come out on the street like he was coming from his house.

Excited now, Rollie scooped up his boots, Rollie pulled them on hopping across the floor on one foot. Stamping his feet to settle them, he grabbed his gun belt, looping it over his shoulder. Trying to hustle and walk softly at the same time, Rollie hurried from the hotel. As he burst out of the hotel, he could see just the faintest traces of light in the eastern sky.

Hoping Moser would be at the Chuck Wagon, getting ready for the morning crowd, Rollie rounded the corner of the hotel, hustling up the alley to the back door of the café. "Hey Moser, open up. Let me in," he called, banging on the door with his fist.

A bleary-eyed Moser swung the door open, rubbing the grizzly stubble on his cheeks. "Rollie, lad, we don't open for another hour. Coffee ain't even ready yet."

"Forget that," Rollie said, shouldering past the old cook. In the center of the room Rollie turned, leaning against a table. "I know who the killer is. One of them anyway."

That snapped Moser's eyes wide open, the makings of a grin tugging at his lips. "Yeah? Who?' he whispered.

"The storekeeper. Burke."

Moser sagged into a chair leaning his elbows on the table, and rubbing the side of his face. "Aw, Rollie, that don't hardly make sense. Joshua wouldn't hurt a fly. I'm, sorry boy, but I can't see it at all."

"Why not?" Rollie demanded.

"Aw, to begin with Burke is kind of a Millie. Like I said, he wouldn't hurt nothing. I don't figure him for killing anybody. He'd be too scared."

Rollie crossed his arms across his chest, glaring down at the old cook. "Yeah? Well, tell me this; how did he get out into the street so fast after Baines was shot tonight?"

Moser shook his head wearily. "He wasn't more than a few seconds ahead of me."

"Are you sure about that? He coulda shot Baines ran down the alley and waited, until he saw folks coming out, then come into the street like he was coming from his house. Did you notice? He was the only one dressed," Rollie argued, watching a shadow of doubt creep across Moser's face. The cook started to argue, but Rollie held up his hand, cutting him off. "Plus did you catch what he said? He said Baines must have seen something out at Diablo Canyon."

"So?" Moser shrugged. "You said the same thing."

"Yeah, but I never said it to him. The only person I told where Baines jumped me was you. So how did Baines know that Claude had been to Diablo Canyon?"

"I dunno. Maybe I told him," Moser said, glumly.

"Did you? Have you even talked to him?"

Suddenly Moser swore, jumping to his feet. "Dang it, man, we gotta be careful with this. Joshua is a well respected man in this town. Liked too. He's staked many a man who was on hard times. We gotta be sure."

"I am sure," Rollie said quickly. "When I was bringing in Baines, I saw Burke, more importantly he saw us."

"Joshua?" Moser said rubbing his chin as he paced. "What in blazes was he doing out of town?"

Rollie shrugged, impatient to get the story out. "Looked like he was delivering supplies to Marge Ross, but that's not what's important right now."

"What is important?"

"The fact that Burke saw me and Baines," Rollie said, pacing now. He and Moser circled each other in the dining room. "See, I kept wondering how Bickerstaff's men got into town so fast. I mean think about it, how'd they even know I had arrested Baines?"

"You're thinking Joshua told them," Moser mused, running a meaty hand up and down the side of his face. "Man they woulda had to run the legs off them horses to get here so fast, but they mighta made it. Course maybe Joshua didn't have to go all the way out to Hank's. Maybe he run into them, when they was coming in off the range. They'd had plenty of time then."

"There you go," Rollie grunted.

Rollie and Moser started circling each other again. Rollie stopped circling, placing his hands on his hips. "Burke is our man. I am sure of that," Rollie said finally. "You got any coffee?"

"No, I done told you it wasn't ready yet," Moser griped.

"You did?"

"Dang sure did!" Moser grunted. "I swear you listen about as well as a bucket of horseshoes." Shaking his head, Moser crossed to the small stove. He opened the iron door, cursing as he burned his fingers. Licking his fingers, the old cook stared critically into the stove. He stirred the embers, blowing the coals and adding a little kindling. Finally deciding the fire was going good, he used the toe of his boot to slam the door shut.

"Rollie we gotta keep this under our hats. Word gets out that we suspect Burke and folks might just take things into their own hands," Moser fretted as he filled the coffee pot with water from a bucket.

"So you believe me about Burke?"

Moser groaned, nodding slightly. "I reckon so," he allowed. "But we gotta go careful. I couldn't ever forgive myself if something happened to him and we found out he wasn't the right man."

Rollie nodded, watching the old cook scoop coffee into the pot. Moser was right. Folks were mad, and they were scared. A quick lynching was a distinct possibility. Rollie knew he wouldn't ever feel right if something happened and they found they were wrong about the storekeeper.

"I'll go out to Diablo Canyon today," Rollie decided. "Whatever is going on, it's tied to something out there. Maybe while I'm gone, you could keep an eye on Burke. Maybe do some snooping."

Moser turned away from the stove, a frown cutting across his florid face. "I just thought of something. Joshua couldn't have killed all those people." Moser dropped heavily into a chair. "He ain't left town in a month of Sundays. Shoot, he's in that store from dawn to dusk. I'd know if it had been closed. And believe me, there ain't any way he'd trust anybody else to run that store. Shoot I bet he counts the money twice cause he don't trust himself."

Rollie shook his head. Moser was just trying to defend his friend. Shoot Burke left town yesterday and Moser didn't notice. Coulda happened a lot. Rollie slid into a chair across from Moser, leaning in close. "Look, I think you are right, Burke didn't shoot those fellas outside of town, but he sure shot Baines. I'm betting he's the one that killed Ben Riggs too."

"Maybe," Moser said. "Dang, Joshua. You think you know somebody."

Whatever else Moser was going to say was cut off by a tapping on the back door. Both of them jumped, snapping their eyes to the back door. Seeing Sarah's face in the window, Rollie felt a thrill shoot through him. The hair on the back of his arms standing up, he grinned sheepishly at Moser, slipping his gun back into his holster. Rollie didn't even remember drawing it. As Moser lumbered to the back door, Rollie settled back into his chair, feeling his heart skip a beat. She looked like an angel, her face framed in the window.

"Come in, missy," Moser boomed, swinging the door wide. "What can we do for you this morning?"

Sarah blushed, shifting her feet, looking past Moser at Rollie. "Oh, I was just going to have some breakfast. Seems like it has been forever since I came down and treated myself to breakfast," she said, speaking very fast.

Moser beamed, looking from her to Rollie. "Sure, sure, we can get you fixed right up. You just sit right here," he said pulling back the chair next to Rollie. "Ethel, we need two breakfasts, pronto."

"Ivan Moser, get your fat backside back here and help me with the cooking!" Ethel yelled from kitchen. She stepped to the door, ready to give Moser the what for, but stopped short seeing Rollie and Sarah. "Oh," she said, and quickly smiled. "Would you two kids like some sweet, flapjacks? I might be persuaded to mix some up."

Rollie shot a quick glance at Sarah, who still blushing gave a small shrug. "Sure, ma'am, that would be great."

"Coming right up," Ethel chirped brightly. "You'll like them. I got a secret ingredient that makes them sweet enough to melt in your mouth."

"She puts a bit of molasses in them," Moser whispered, but his wife heard him.

"Ivan Moser! That's a secret," she yelled throwing a wet dish towel at him. She stamped her foot as he easily caught the towel. Hands on hips, she scowled mightily at her husband. "Ivan get yourself back here and help me."

"Yeah, yeah, I'm coming," he growled, as he struggled out of the chair. Before leaving, Moser leaned into Rollie, whispering loudly. "I think she likes you, boy. This is the first time she ever came in for breakfast.

With a wink at Sarah, the old cook lumbered into the kitchen to help his wife. Rollie squirmed in his chair, embarrassed because he knew Sarah had heard the old cook. "Ah, well, I'm real glad you decided to come for breakfast," he stammered. He pulled at his collar, wishing he had washed up a little before coming down. Man it was hot in here. Dang ol' Moser, he musta thrown most of a tree in that stove, Rollie thought, feeling sweat trickle down his back.

"Thank you," Sarah said, her face shinning bright red. She looked up from the table, and into Rollie's eyes. "Mister Moser is right though, I did want to see you," she said, taking a deep breath. "I need to tell you something."

"Oh," Rollie said, feeling a crushing wave of disappointment roll over him. She didn't want to have breakfast with him; she wanted to talk to the sheriff. "What did you need to say?" he asked, trying to keep the disappointment out of his voice.

Sarah quickly dropped her eyes, talking to the red-checkered table cloth. "Rebecca Moreland isn't who she says she is."

"What? How do you know that?" Moser asked, approaching the table with a coffee pot and two cups.

"Because Rebecca Moreland died of cholera about six years ago. I know, I was her roommate in school. I was there."

"No foolin'," Moser said dropping the coffee pot on the table and dropping into a chair. "But Jim and Mort got all them letters from her. They've been getting them all this time. Shoot I even seen some of them."

Sarah dropped her head a fraction lower. "I know, I wrote all of those. My folks died in the epidemic, and I had no money. When the money and the letters kept coming for Becky, well, I used the money to stay in school, and then started writing them back."

Moser whistled softly, shaking his head. "Oh man, Mort's gonna be heart broke. He set store by them letters."

"He already knows," Rollie said, snagging the coffee pot. With the pot poised over the two cups, he paused, looking at Sarah. "Doesn't he?"

Sarah raised her head, meeting Rollie's eyes and nodding. "How did you know?"

Rollie poured the coffee, shrugging. "I didn't, but something about Mort's reaction when I told him she was in town has been bothering me. So when you told me she wasn't the real Rebecca Moreland, I figured he knew."

Sarah nodded, taking the coffee Rollie offered. "Jim and Mort came back east last year for our graduation. I met them at the station and told them the whole story."

"That sure musta took some gumption," Moser whistled again, snagging the other cup right out of Rollie's hand. "Bet they was mad."

Sarah gave him a weak smile. "Not as much as I feared." She blew out a sigh. "I was so scared waiting on them to get there, several times I almost ran out." She paused taking a small sip from the cup. "But they were great. They came to the graduation. They even took me out to eat in this really fancy place." A wistful smile crept on to her face as she recalled that night. "We got all dressed up and went to this fancy place. They had these fancy teacups and little cakes, it was so perfect."

Rollie shook his head, trying to call up an image of Mort all slicked up, and couldn't quite do it. "Mort had some business to do, so they stayed almost a week. They bought me some new clothes, and then they told me they would give me the money to buy the hotel if I would come here."

"That was nice of them," Rollie commented, not knowing what else to say.

"I thought so," Sarah replied.

"So that's why Mort didn't want me to just hand the ranch over to Rebecca," Rollie said, thinking out loud.

"I guess so," Sarah said, and managed a smile. She let out a small sigh. "It sure feels good to get that off my chest. I feel like I have been lying to everyone this whole time."

Moser beamed at her, covering her small dainty hand with his huge, rough one. "Don't you fret over it, missy. Reckon everyone has a few secrets they'd like to keep locked away."

As Moser turned his eyes to Rollie, the sheriff gave a small start. Did Moser know the truth? Maybe it was time to come clean. Suddenly Rollie wanted to tell Sarah the truth. Let her know, she wasn't the only one who had regrets. "I haven't been exactly honest myself," he blurted out.

"Aw crud," Moser groaned, hitching his chair closer. "Rollie, what did you do? I gotta tell you, folks ain't exactly happy with you right now."

"Is it as bad as what I did?" Sarah asked, laying her hand on his.

"Worse," Rollie said, feeling a lump in his throat and a trip in his heartbeat. "You know when I said I came here to kill Claude Baines because he shot me and stole my horse?"

"Yeah," Moser said, drawing the word out. "That ain't true?"

"No, I lied about that."

"Oh no," Moser groaned, slapping his forehead. "Aw, man, folks were really peeved that the first thing you done after becoming sheriff was chase down Baines, but since they figured you had a really good reason, they were willing to forgive and forget. But now?"

"Arresting Baines wasn't the first thing I did," Rollie protested. "And even when I arrested him, I wasn't looking for him. I was tracking the feller that shot Bickerstaff's man." Rollie paused, just like last night in the sheriff's office; something was in the back of his mind, trying to come forward. "Baines did try to kill me, that's why I arrested him," Rollie added slowly, his mind trying to figure out what he was missing.

"So you say, but we only got your say so on that," Moser shot back.

"You saw my rifle."

"Coulda done that yourself," Moser countered. "Look, Rollie, my boy, I like you, but you gotta look at it the way folks in town are gonna see it. You admit you already lied to us once, now we're supposed to believe you. Gonna be hard to sell."

"Why did you come here after Baines?" Sarah asked softly.

"Yeah, that," Rollie said, rubbing the side of his face, starting to wish he'd not brought this up. "It all started several years back. I was sixteen and out on my own for the first time. I don't know. I guess I wanted to be a bad man. Prove to everybody how tough I was."

"Reckon a lot of young fellers go through that. I know I did. Just got to get it outta your system," Moser said, with a wise nod of his head.

"You men. I don't know why you think you have to be so tough," Sarah scolded, but she softened it with a smile.

"I don't know either," Rollie said, returning the smile, then turning serious. "But at that time, I sure wanted to show everybody that I was tough. Anyway, it was fall and I had been down in Texas working all summer and was riding the grub line heading back home."

As he talked, Rollie could still picture it; even smell the dust in the air from that summer. "One evening I rode into this little town in north Texas. Course I felt like I had to go to the saloon for a drink. Well, I had my drink and a few more. I fell in with this rough crowd. They were talking about going out and killing this fella Joe Turner. They were saying Turner was wanted and there was a reward."

"Was he wanted?" Sarah asked, sounding a little breathless.

"No. He was just some guy trying to make a ranch out of some dusty piece of ground. He'd had words with this big rancher. The words turned into a fight and Turner whipped him good. This rancher's son takes a shot at Turner, misses, but Turner shoots him."

"Kill him?" Moser asked, gravely.

"No, but the rancher put a bounty on Turner's head. These fellas I was drinking with they were gonna go collect the bounty. Now at the time, I thought them fellas was tough, but looking back, I see they were drinking to get their nerve up. After a bunch of drinks, three of us decide to go see Turner. Baines was kinda the leader and on the way out, he decides I should be the one to face Turner. Being so young, I didn't know how to say no. I remember feeling trapped by the whole thing. But when we get out there, they hang back in the dark and I ride up, hollering at Turner."

"Were you scared?" Sarah asked.

"Yeah, a little bit, but I was more afraid I might lose my nerve."

"What happened? You kill Turner?" Moser demanded impatiently.

"No, I didn't," Rollie replied shaking his head. "I remember it so clear, seeing Turner looking out the window. He came out to face me and the minute he stepped through the door, Baines shot him. Never even gave him a chance."

Rollie hung his head, staring into the blackness of his coffee, but seeing the scene from so many years ago. "I was sick over it. I just kept looking at Turner and I couldn't believe he was dead."

"I turned around and road out of there. I rode most of the night, trying to get away from it. But I couldn't. Over the years I guess I began to hate Claude Baines and when I heard he was here, I decided to kill him."

"Don't know why you didn't," Moser growled. "I sure woulda."

"Don't listen to him," Sarah said softly, shooting a look at Moser. "I'm glad you didn't."

"Yeah," Rollie grunted swirling his coffee then taking a drink. "I sure thought I wanted to but when it came right down to it, I couldn't do it."

"Ivan, get in here. I've got the flapjacks ready to cook," Ethel called from the kitchen.

"Yeah, yeah, I'll be in there in a minute."

Ethel came to the door leading back into the kitchen. She held a big spoon, dripping batter. Placing a hand on her hip, she pointed the spoon at her husband. "Moser," she said, her voice quiet, as she motioned with the spoon.

Moser grumbled under his breath as he pushed back his chair. "Dang woman, I swear, one of these days."

Ethel smiled sweetly at him. "Yeah, one of these days. But not today, today you get yourself back there and get to cooking."

"I should stay out there," Moser whispered once they were in the kitchen. "I mean Rollie's a right nice fella and pretty smart, but when it comes to sparking, he's about as good as a wet saddle blanket. Reckon I should stay out there and kinda smooth things along."

Ethel snorted, rolling her eyes. "And pray tell just what do you know about sparking? When was the last time you took me anywhere?"

Moser grinned, sweeping his wife up in his arms. "Why we went dancing out a Sutter's party just last fall," he said, spinning her around the kitchen.

Ethel smiled at the memory, pressing up against her husband. "And as I recall, you ended up spending half the night in that poker game," she scolded, but there was a note of humor ringing in her voice.

"Made five bucks," Moser countered with a wide smile. "Bought you that winter shawl you'd been eyeing." He said, kissing her lightly.

Ethel smiled. "Yes you did," she agreed laying her head against his chest, letting him push her around the kitchen. She felt a satisfied smile tug at her lips. The man danced like a drunken bear, but she did love him. She patted him lightly on the chest, and pushed away. "Now, get over there and make them flapjacks."

"You sure, I still think I should get out there, make sure things go good." Moser grinned, rubbing his hands together. "That Rollie boy is just the feller we need to run the freighting end of things. Man if that gal could get him corralled up, he'd never leave."

Ethel peeked around the corner, grinning at Rollie and Sarah. The two were setting very close, their heads together, almost touching. "I think they can get by without you."

"Well, I'll be," Moser said, looking over her shoulder. He was grinning from ear to ear as he turned to his stove. If anything could settle Rollie down and keep him in town, it would be Sarah. Nothing like a pretty girl to get a man thinking about his future.

Moser whistled softly as he spooned the flapjacks into the hot skillet. There was money to be made here, and with a man like Rollie helping him? In his head, he began to recalculate the profits. They'd be rich.

Rollie and Sarah stepped from the café stopping on the boardwalk. They stood shoulder to shoulder, admiring the morning.

"Pretty day," Rollie said, trying to think of something more clever to say, but pretty day was all he came up with.

"It's going to be a nice day," Sarah said, softly. They stood in silence for a few heartbeats, each of them struggling for the right words. Finally, Sarah sighed. "It is going to be a nice day, but it doesn't mean I don't have work to do. I better go get started."

"I'll walk you," Rollie said. "I was thinking, maybe one of these days, we could get a basket and go for a picnic."

"I would like that," Sarah said, her voice soft as a summer breeze. She slipped her small, soft hand inside Rollie's big, rough one. "Maybe Saturday."

"Sure. I'll see if Hartshorn has a buggy we could use."

"I'll get a basket ready."

"That'll be nice," Rollie mumbled, as they reached the hotel. He didn't know if he was supposed to kiss her or not. He knew he wanted to. But he hesitated, and then the moment was gone, passed him by like a twig floating down a stream.

Sarah started inside, hesitating just a second. "So, Saturday then?"

Rollie nodded, feeling a blush crawl up his neck. "Yes, ma'am."

"See you then," Sarah said, and disappeared inside.

Rollie watched her go, feeling like a fool. He kicked himself a little. Man he hadn't done that right. Mumbling to himself, Rollie turned, heading down the street for his horse. He'd taken several steps, mad at himself, before it hit him. He was going on a picnic!

Right away the sweat started trickling down his back. They were going on a picnic. How long did that take. It'd be a spell. Rollie's breakfast began to swim around in his stomach. What was he gonna say. That was a long time. He glanced down at his battered clothing. He had some money. Maybe he should get some new duds. Maybe a suit?

Rollie scowled at the ground. He hated wearing a suit. He'd only had one in his whole life. That was when he was younger and his mother made him wear it to church. He hated that.

Course, women, now, they liked that sort of thing. Maybe he should get one.

Hartshorn looked up from his work, smiling as Rollie wandered into the barn. He'd seen Rollie walk Sarah down the street and recognized that dazed look for what it was. "You look like a man with something on his mind," he commented.

"Yeah," Rollie said, gravely. "Thinking about buying a suit."

Hartshorn smiled. If Rollie was thinking of a suit, the man had it bad. "She's a right fine young lady. Hard worker." Hartshorn grinned at Rollie. "Mighty pretty, too."

"Yeah," Rollie said, rubbing his hands together.

The smith smiled. Funny how a woman could make a man's hands so clammy and sticky. The smith was still smiling as Rollie wandered out of the barn, angling towards the store. Gonna buy that suit, the smith thought. Still grinning, he picked up his hammer, ready to return to his work. The smile slid from his face as he saw Rollie stop in the middle of the street, slipping the thong off his gun. Swearing, the smith grabbed his rifle.

CHAPTER EIGHT

They came into town with a rush, bent low over their saddles. Rollie heard the smith cursing behind him and a door somewhere up the street bang. Stepping to the middle of the street, Rollie snapped a quick shot, saw it miss and fired again.

This time he saw a rider flinch, then right himself in the saddle. The whole street seemed to explode in gunfire as the townsfolk opened up. The riders stopped, milling in the middle of the street, dust boiling up from their horses hooves.

Through the dust, Rollie caught a quick glimpse of Lang, fired a quick shot, knew it was a miss as soon as he pulled the trigger. The riders let loose a ragged volley, then wheeled their horses and fled the town.

Rollie let them go, calmly reloading his gun. "What was that all about?" the smith wondered, his voice a little shaky.

"Guess they didn't like Baines getting killed," Rollie answered, dropping the pistol into the holster.

"You think they will be back?" Moser asked trudging up the street, his rifle still ready.

"No, I don't think so," Rollie said, with a slow shake of his head. "Wasn't much of a raid."

"I dunno, I'm still shaking." Moser blew out a sigh. "But you are right; they didn't seem all that serious about it. It was like they just wanted to come to town, fire a few shots and get the heck outta here."

Rollie nodded, thinking it over. It wasn't like the town had put up a real fight. Just the three of them firing up the street. Like Moser said, the raiders seemed to be content with blasting off a few shots. It was like Lang had just been going through the motions.

"Where's Joshua?" Hartshorn wondered, cutting across Rollie's thoughts.

"Yeah where the devil is he?" Moser grunted looking up and down the street. "Ain't like him to miss something like this."

It was Sarah who found him halfway down the five foot wide walkway between the hotel and the general store. He lay in a half-sitting position against the wall of the hotel, a crisp bullet hole punched through the left side of his starched shirt. Sarah Eckles stood at the entrance to the walkway, a hand over her mouth.

"Is he dead?" she asked, and from the horrified look on her face, Rollie figured she knew the answer before she even asked the question.

Rollie knelt beside him, knowing there wasn't much hope. Judging from the looks of the bullet hole, the shot took him in the heart. "Yeah, he's dead," Rollie said, after checking him.

"Poor Joshua," Hartshorn said sadly. "Guess he was just standing in the wrong place at the wrong time." A horrified look sprang to Hartshorn's beefy face. "Oh dear Lord, I hope it wasn't one of us who shot him. I mean we were all firing….," Hartshorn's words died away as he swallowed hard. He didn't even want to think about such a thing.

The big smith's words clicked something in Rollie's mind. Everything that had been worrying away at his brain, suddenly locked into focus. "I don't think so. This was no accident. This man was murdered."

"What?" Hartshorn sputtered, seconds ahead of Moser and Sarah.

"Why would anyone want to kill poor Mister Burke?" Sarah asked.

"I'll explain it later," Rollie said, rising swiftly to his feet. "I want to check on something. I'll meet you at the café in a few minutes."

Rollie didn't bother to wait for an answer, he took off down the walkway towards the rear of the building, his eyes sweeping the ground for tracks and there were plenty. Everyone used this walkway, cutting between the buildings instead of walking around.

He could hear Hartshorn and Moser grunting as they hefted Burke's body off the ground, carrying him over to the stable, where he would be kept until they could bury him.

Rollie saw a few smudges which looked fresh, but nothing that he could use. At the rear of the buildings, Rollie paused, wondering which way the killer would take. In an instant, he knew the killer would turn right and head south, down past the stable. Not only was that the fastest way out of town, it was also away from where everyone was gathering.

Turning right, Rollie moved slowly, weaving back and forth, casting for tracks. Halfway across the breath of the hotel, he saw what he was looking for. A track in the dust. Immediately, Rollie recognized it for what it was; the track of a man in moccasins, moving fast. Rollie could even see where the toes had dug into the softer dirt behind the store. Rollie stared at the track, trying to guess the size of the man wearing it, but it was only the front part of the foot. Rollie could see where his foot had slid making the track look wider. Giving up, Rollie continued down the walkway.

At the far corner of the hotel, he saw where a horse had been tied. The horse had small, dainty feet. This horse wasn't a plow horse, with small feet like that, he would be a runner.

The horse had done some shifting around but not a lot. Rollie judged he had been tied there twenty minutes, maybe a bit longer, but certainly not more than forty minutes. He found a few stray strands of gray hair stuck to the corner of the hotel. Other than himself, Rollie hadn't seen anyone riding a gray horse, but that didn't mean much. Lots of folks had more than one horse. And if the killer was using one, a gray to do his killing, it stood to reason he would keep the animal out of sight the rest of the time.

Pushing the hair into his shirt pocket, Rollie glanced back down at the ground. The horse had taken out fast. For a second, Rollie considered trying to track the horse, but then changed his mind. He knew the rider could hide his trail and Rollie figured he could trail the man, but it would take forever and there was no need. Rollie knew who the killer was.

Rollie walked over to the café, gathering his thoughts. Several people were gathered around the tables as Rollie pushed through the door. "Well, I reckon this tells us Joshua wasn't the killer," Moser said, passing Rollie a cup of coffee, and replacing the pot on the stove. "Dad burn it, boy. You almost had me going. I was actually starting to believe Joshua was mixed up in this."

"Oh, I don't know," Rollie said, taking a sip of the coffee.

Sarah Eckles had been blowing into her cup, now she glanced over the rim at Rollie. "You mean you actually thought Mister Burke was involved in the killings?"

"I did." Rollie nodded grimly. "Now I'm sure of it."

A quick frown marred Sarah's pretty features. "That seems difficult to believe. Mister Burke always seemed so nice."

Marge Ross snorted loudly. "Well, I can sure believe it," Marge boomed, breezing through the doorway like a hurricane. "If you ask me, he was a mean son of a bucket."

Hartshorn grimaced, started to look up, then became very interested in his coffee. "Please, Ms Ross, the man is dead."

"I don't care if he's dead or dancing a jig, the man was greedier than an outhouse rat." Marge plopped down in a chair, which popped and groaned under her weight. "There sure weren't any bargains to be found in that store of his, and I reckon if he didn't have to sleep he wouldn't have ever closed." Marge swung her hard, calculating eyes to Rollie. "You reckon he was involved in all this nonsense?"

"Yes, I do, and I don't think his death was any accident."

"You said that before," Moser pointed out, scratching the point of his chin. "What makes you think that? I mean there was a pile of shooting going on. If you ask me it was a miracle that more folks weren't hit."

"Hush. Let the boy speak his mind," Marge instructed. "I'd say he's got something to say that might be worth hearing."

"Sure, there were a lot of bullets flying, but none of them were really fired in the direction of the store and the hotel. Plus he was fifteen feet back from the street and that walkway is mighty narrow."

"Bullet could have punched right through the building," Moser offered. "I've seen it before.

"Wasn't any holes in the buildings," Rollie countered. "I know, I looked. I don't see how a bullet could have gotten back there."

Blank faces stared back at Rollie, all except for Marge Ross. She looked like a fox who just realized the hen house door was left open. "What are you thinking happened then?" she asked, her voice almost gentle.

Rollie swirled his coffee, trying to corral all the stray thoughts running through his mind and put them into words. "The raid on the town, I kept coming back to that. Those boys didn't put up much of a fight. We all noticed that." Rollie paused, looking at the faces gathered around the table, surprised at the attentive respect he saw. Rollie was used to being respected for what he could do, for what he knew about horses and guns, but not for what he thought. It kinda threw him. "I was thinking…, ah well, I was thinking that the raid was a bluff. Get us looking somewhere else so somebody could slip into town and kill Burke."

Hartshorn sat his cup on the table, wrapping his big, rough hands around it as he leaned his elbows on the table. "Why would anyone want to kill Joshua?"

"I've been thinking, everything points out to Diablo Canyon. I think Mort Killigan found gold there. Likely a lot of it and that is what this whole thing is all about."

Rollie took a sip of coffee, watching their faces. They wanted to believe there was gold. They were all good honest people, but their first thoughts were if there really was gold, they might be able to get some of it.

"So Mort found gold at Diablo Canyon?" Moser mused, already trying to figure out a way to make money off it.

Rollie nodded. "Now that canyon, it cuts across land owned by his brother, so Mort doesn't bother to file his claim since he's not overly worried about ownership. I figure Mort knew if he filed a claim, word would get around and soon everybody would know he hit the big one. He didn't want that. He tried to keep it quiet, but someone found out about the gold."

"You're talking about Joshua?" Moser interrupted.

Rollie shook his head. "Maybe, but I don't think so. I think it was Bickerstaff."

"If that is true, why would Mister Bickerstaff kill all those people and not Mort Killigan?" Sarah asked, concentration knotting up her smooth features.

"Couldn't just up and snuff old Mort. Everybody would know about the gold. I mean Mort is harmless, only one reason anybody would want to kill him," Moser said, growing excitement in his tone.

"Yeah, but who would miss him," Hartshorn argued. "He could kill Mort and hide the body and no one would think much about it. Lots of times its months between times Mort comes into town. If he never showed up, folks would just think something happened."

"There is that," Rollie agreed, nodding at the smith. "But I think the real reason he didn't kill Mort first is because it would do him no good. Look at it from Bickerstaff's point of view. He wants the gold, but even if he kills Mort, he still has a problem."

"The gold is on Jim Killigan's ranch," Ethel Moser said, carrying three plates with a slice of pie on each one from the kitchen.

"Say, that's right," Ivan Moser agreed, reaching greedily for one of the plates. "Bickerstaff couldn't work the claim as long as old Jim Killigan was alive," he added, scowling as his wife pulled the pie from his reach and set it in front of Marge Ross, Sarah and Hartshorn.

"Yeah, so the first thing he does is take Jim Killigan out of the way," Rollie said absently, as he watched Ethel return to the kitchen. "I reckon he figures he can get rid of Mort any time," Rollie added, hoping she had more pie in the kitchen.

"I reckon you're onto something there, boy," Marge said, cutting off a huge piece of her pie and forking it into her mouth. "But you can bet your aching backside that he wants Killigan's ranch, too," she mumbled around the pie.

"But, what about the other? Been a passel of folks sent to meet their makers," Moser argued, sulking. Rollie shrugged, he didn't have it all figured out.

"Why would you assume it was Bickerstaff? Wouldn't Tinsworth be just as likely?" Sarah asked.

"The sheriff was killed on Bickerstaff's property." Rollie paused herding his thoughts. "Everyone thinks the sheriff was killed because he found something out. I reckon he did, and then he faced Bickerstaff with it. Hank likely denied it, then followed the sheriff and killed him. As for the rest, I figure Hank was keeping a close eye on that canyon and killed anyone he caught out there poking around."

"What about Joshua?" Moser asked his face lighting up as his wife came out of the kitchen with more pie. "How does he fit in all of this then?"

"Well, I'm not really sure how it all happened." Rollie admitted, grinning at Ethel Moser as she set a piece of pie in front of him. "Maybe Burke found out about the gold first and went to Bickerstaff for help. But more than likely, I figure Burke found out what Bickerstaff was up to and demanded to cut in."

"I don't know," Moser said beaming from ear to ear as his wife placed the last piece of pie in front of him. "I'd say Hank just killed him right then and there."

Rollie looked longingly down at his pie. He dearly wanted to dig in, but figured he best get this story out while it was all still straight in his mind. "Yeah, most times, you likely would be right, but this time Bickerstaff needed Burke, or at least someone who lived in town."

"Ben Riggs," Hartshorn said a note of sadness in his voice.

"Yeah, Bickerstaff couldn't hardly get at Riggs without being seen in town and he wouldn't want to risk that," Rollie explained.

"Ah, so he played along with Burke and Burke killed poor old Ben Riggs," Marge said, nodding her head like she was pumping water.

Without thinking, Rollie found himself nodding along with her. "I figure Burke was the one who killed Claude Baines in jail. I figure Bickerstaff told him that Baines had been nosing around out at Diablo Canyon and he found out about the gold so, he had to be eliminated."

"That's why Joshua was the only one dressed when we all got out in the street that night!" Moser sputtered his mouth full of pie.

"We all assumed he came from his house in the back of the store, but all he did was run down the alley then come out between the buildings. Same place he was killed."

Sarah had been picking daintily at her pie and now she looked up, her eyes large. "But why would Mister Bickerstaff kill Mister Burke? They were partners after all."

"Cause Hank is a greedy son of a slop bucket!" Marge Ross boomed, dropping her fork into her empty plate and shoving it away. She leaned back, sighing as she patted her stomach. "You can bet your cash against a pile of horse manure that he don't intend to share with anyone."

"Do you think that Bickerstaff had Baines killed just so his men would have an excuse to raid the town? Sounds like a lot of planning and trouble to go through," Hartshorn asked, clearly worried about a fellow human being who was that devious and cold blooded.

"Hank always was a smart devil," Marge said shortly. Moser said, reaching for Sarah's plate as she pushed it away. "You gonna finish that, missy?"

Her face pale, Sarah shook her head. "I'm not hungry," she replied, then smiled a tiny smile as Moser drug the plate over so he could finish her pie. "But I mean killing Ben Riggs. That is cold. Bickerstaff is a hard man. Maybe he could kill Ben, but Joshua? I can't believe he could do it."

"I don't know," Ethel Moser said taking a piece of pie for herself. "I never quite trusted him. He could be pretty salty."

They all talked some more, but nothing came of it. Rollie quickly realized that the thought of Mort finding gold was clouding their judgment. They were good people, but they all wanted a piece of the gold.

Rollie left the café, wondering what to do next. He needed to have a talk with Mort. The old prospector moved around a good bit, he would know more about what was going on than anybody.

Maybe the first thing he should do is put a whoa to Tinsworth. Rollie paused leaning against the awning in front of the hotel, staring at Tinsworth's saloon.

Maybe he should go talk to the banker. If Rollie had things figured right, Tinsworth hadn't really killed anybody. Not yet He'd sent his men out to harass the settlers, but that had been about it. Lots of places nobody would even think twice about that. If the farmers couldn't hold their land, then they didn't deserve it.

Still it would be best to put a stop to it. He needed to do something anyway. Rollie could feel the townspeople's eyes on him. They were watching, waiting for him to do something. To set things right. Time to do it.

His mind made up, Rollie pushed away from the awning, heading for the saloon. As he walked, Rollie began to feel better. Just doing something helped. Might not be right, but it was something.

Rollie knew that even though Tinsworth owned the bank, he spent most of his time in the saloon. Truthfully, it felt good to be doing something. Rollie didn't care for Tinsworth; the banker just rubbed him wrong. And he was getting mad. Rollie liked Swenson and the others. He'd enjoy jacking the banker up.

At the door, Rollie paused, slipping the thongs off his guns. This might get messy. With a deep breath, Rollie pushed through the door. The saloon was almost empty. Bob Neal the bartender stood behind the bar and Carney lounged at a table, kicked back in his chair, his feet resting on the table.

Carney gave a start as Rollie entered, but as Rollie glared at him, he settled back into his chair. Rollie branded Carney with a long stare then turned to Neal who had been adding water to half full whiskey bottles. Now the bartender stood frozen, a glass poised above the bottle.

"I'm here to see Tinsworth. Law business." Rollie let his hand fall to his gun, pinning Neal with a stern look. "Am I gonna have any trouble from you?"

"No, sir."

"Good," Rollie grunted. "Might be a good time for you to visit the privy."

"Yeah," Neal agreed his head bobbing up and down like a pump handle. "I am feeling the urge all of a sudden."

Rollie watched him scurry from behind the bar, then out the door. When Neal was gone, Rollie slid his gaze to Carney. "Thought I told you to leave the country?"

Carney shrugged, spreading his hands and trying a slick grin, but it didn't quite come off. "Thought I'd stay," he said, his voice croaking a mite.

"Where's Tinsworth?"

"Don't know, he ain't here. I was waiting for him." Carney told the lie smoothly enough, but Rollie saw his eyes flick to a door in the back of the room.

"Is that right?" Rollie said softly, and then sprang across the room. Carney tried to react, but his feet being on the table slowed him. He swept his feet off the table and jumped to his feet.

His gun was just coming out when Rollie grabbed him. Ignoring the gun Rollie yanked the gunman out of his chair. Pivoting on his heels, Rollie took two long steps and slung Carney across the room, sending him crashing into the door. Carney hit that door head long and went through it like it wasn't even there, leaving a trail of splinters.

Following right behind him, Rollie saw Carney bounce off a desk and crash into the floor. Behind the desk a startled Tinsworth swore, trying to come to his feet. Rollie slammed into the desk shoving it back pinning the banker back against the wall. Tinsworth swore, struggling to push the desk away. "Shut up and sit still," Rollie growled, glancing sideways at Carney. The gunman was laying on the floor a trickle of blood running across his face. For good measure, Rollie gave him a solid boot to the ribs, and then turned back to Tinsworth.

"What is the meaning of this?" Tinsworth sputtered, trying to take control of the situation.

"Shut up and listen," Rollie growled, leaning against the desk, grinning as the big desk cut off Tinsworth's air. "I'm here to set things right," Rollie said, easing off the desk and letting the banker breath. "You lay off those farmers. They own that land fair and square. I hear that you been bothering them again and I'll come back and shove this desk down your throat."

"You're taking in a lot of territory."

Tinsworth's words ended in a bleat as Rollie slammed the desk back into his mid-section. "You just let me worry about that," Rollie said, grinning down at the banker. "You stay away from Jim Killigan's place. That belongs to Mort."

"Hey, I have legal claim to that," Tinsworth said, snatching a piece of paper from his desk, and shaking it at Rollie. "His niece signed it over to me this morning."

"Yeah?" Rollie said, snatching the paper from Tinsworth's fingers. Rollie glanced at it then wadded it into a ball and tossed it back at Tinsworth. "Best take that over to the outhouse; I bet Neal can use it about now. That's all it's good for."

Tinsworth sneered up at Rollie. "Don't worry, it's legal, Jim's niece signed it."

"You mean that girl staying at the hotel?" Rollie demanded and Tinsworth nodded a calculating look coming to his face. "Well she ain't no more related to Jim Killigan than you are. I don't know where you dug her up, but she ain't his niece, I happen to know the real Rebecca Killigan died years ago."

"What about the note I have that Jim signed?" Tinsworth protested."He borrowed a lot of money from me."

"I doubt that," Rollie said shrugging. "But that is between you and Mort. He can pay you if he wants, but personally, I'd tell you where to go."

Rollie cut across country heading for Diablo Canyon. Mort would likely be there, and if not, Rollie felt sure that he could find the claim.

If nothing else, it would be nice to know that he was tracking down the right trail. If Mort had found gold, then everything else kinda made some sense. If not? Then he was back to the beginning.

Rollie took his time, watching his back trail. He could feel an itch coming on between his shoulder blades. Too many had already been killed, and Rollie felt no desire to join them. Looping wide, Rollie approached the canyon. Riding up to the edge, he could see the marks in the dirt where he had gone over the edge after Baines shot him.

Baines? Now there was a question. Why had he been here? He was a ways from Bickerstaff's range. No reason for him to be here. Nothing to do with the ranch anyway.

Rollie pushed back his hat. Had Baines found out about the gold? Baines was a sneaky sort, with a nose for easy money. It'd be just like him to know about the gold. Pondering the situation, Rollie swung down, prowling the top looking for an easy way down.

Course maybe Bickerstaff had sent Baines out here to watch over the place, keep strangers away. Made sense that if Bickerstaff knew about the gold that he'd want to keep folks away.

What didn't make sense is why would he send Baines. Baines was a new man. Made more sense that he would send one of his older men. Someone he knew he could trust. Shoot maybe he didn't have anybody he could trust.

Rollie recalled hearing something about Lang and Baines being old riding buddies. Lang was Bickerstaff's right hand man, his foreman. Maybe Lang had vouched for Baines.

Rollie was still mulling it over when he found what he was looking for. Not a way to the bottom, but the claim itself. At least a spot where somebody had been digging. As he approached, a frown snuck onto Rollie's face. He didn't know a lot about mining, but he hadn't expected to find the claim up here on the flat. Rollie had been picturing a shaft sunk into the bank, down by the water.

As he approached the hole, Rollie's frown deepened to a full grown scowl. The hole was only about three feet square and a foot or so deep. It just didn't seem right, if Mort were pulling gold outta here, the hole should be bigger. Way bigger. And if Rollie had things figured right, Mort had been taking gold outta here for a good while. When he and Jim went back east to see Sarah, she said Mort had money. That he'd bought her things. Rollie scuffed the bottom of the hole with the toe of his boot. The dirt was cracked and weathered; it'd been a good while since anyone had dug here. And where was the tailings? It almost looked as if somebody had dug the hole, then carried off the dirt. Why?

This wasn't the claim.

The only good thing that come of finding the hole was just past the hole was a well worn trail going to the bottom. Leading the gray, Rollie took the trial to the bottom.

At the bottom, Rollie stopped short, the gray bumping into him. What the devil was that?

A few feet from the water sat a strange structure. Turning the gray loose to get a drink, Rollie cocked his head studying the thing. Looked like a big oven.

Aw shoot, it was. Rollie smiled. This was the kiln Swenson built to bake the mud bricks.

Rollie squatted down next to the remains of a fire. He could see where they had mixed the clay with water shaping the bricks for the kiln, and then cooked them over the open fire. Rollie smiled again. Now things made some sense.

Now he knew why Jim had halted the making of the mud bricks for the silos.

Mort's claim had to be right close.

Rolling a smoke, Rollie let it sift through his mind. It sure did seem that Mort had never actually told his brother where his claim was located. So Jim sets up a kiln to cook his mud bricks right here. Rollie chuckled a little trying to imagine Mort's reaction when Swenson and his buddies showed up here and started making bricks. Bet ol' Mort made a brick of his own, Rollie thought, letting out a dry chuckle.

Mort had likely burned the grass riding over to Jim's place. Once he told Jim the lay of things, Jim put a hold on the brick building. That explained Jim's secrecy about stopping the building. Then before Jim could come up with a new place to build the bricks someone up and killed him. That riled Rollie more than a little. He had never met Jim Killigan, but he felt like he would have liked the old man.

Straightening up, Rollie looked both ways. The gold claim had to be real close.

As many times as Rollie had told himself that he didn't care about the gold, Rollie couldn't help himself. He felt the excitement of being so close to a fortune tugging at him. Aw shoot, wouldn't hurt nothing to do a little poking around. Telling himself that, Rollie stated scouring the canyon for signs of the claim.

After just a few minutes, Rollie came on some tracks. Squatting on his heels, Rollie studied the tracks. They were fresh. Certainly made in the last twenty- four hours, and likely made that day. The tracks were smears in the soft sandy ground, making it hard to tell if he had ever seen them before.

Who made the tracks was impossible to tell, but what they were doing was plain as day. They had done exactly what Rollie was doing, Looking for Mort's gold. The tracks criss crossed the bottom of the canyon as the unknown rider checked both sides. He'd spent some time looking for the mine.

And he never found it.

Rollie saw where the guy had gave up, jumping his horse up out of the canyon. Curious, Rollie followed the tracks up out of the canyon, and then trailed as they led away from the canyon.

The tracks were easy to follow, as the man was hustling. Rollie grinned. Whoever this man was, he'd spent too much time looking for the gold, and now he was in a powerful hurry.

Hustling a little himself, Rollie followed the tracks for an hour. After just a little bit, it became apparent that the rider was heading towards Bickerstaff's ranch. Bickerstaff himself? Or one of his men? Rollie wondered.

At the end of the hour, Rollie saw where the rider met up with another group of men driving a small herd of cattle. By now, Rollie was sure they were already onto Bickerstaff's range. The rider fell in with the group, still heading for Bickerstaff's home.

Deciding there wasn't any use to follow, Rollie turned his horse around, going back to Diablo Canyon. He felt certain he knew where the rider was going, Bickerstaff's place, but it might be helpful to know where he came from.

At the canyon, Rollie picked up the trail. As before the rider had been moving fast, and looked to be coming from town.

Rollie frowned. He'd almost outsmarted himself today. By looping wide when he left town and watching his back trail for someone following him, Rollie had completely missed these tracks. If he hadn't stayed to look for the claim, he woulda completely missed this. Just luck that he found these tracks. Rollie had to grin a little. Sometimes better to be lucky than good.

As the afternoon slipped into evening, Rollie followed the trail, leading straight back to town. In the dim light, Rollie almost missed it. The rider hadn't come from town, he come from the direction of Marge Ross's place. He could see where tracks came from the direction of Marge Ross's place and met the raiders' right here.

As darkness crept in, Rollie leaned back in the saddle, rolling a smoke. He was pretty sure it hadn't been Marge Ross out at the canyon. He grinned a little at the thought of her wasting part of a day looking for a gold mine.

She wasn't the type to encourage visitors either. So why had the rider come from her place? In a flash, Rollie knew he hadn't. This was the man that shot Joshua Burke. If the rider had cut straight out of town behind the livery, he woulda been headed right for Marge's place.

Made some sense. If it were Bickerstaff who snuffed Burke, he wouldn't want to take a chance on meeting anybody on the trail. By cutting across country, and circling around behind Marge's place he'd be out of sight until he was well clear of town.

It all kinda fit. Bickerstaff needed to get Burke outta the way. So he sends his men to shoot up the town, keeping everyone busy while he slips in and deals with Burke. Then he snuck out of town the back way and meets up with his crew here. Bickerstaff gives them their orders and then headed to Diablo Canyon to look for the gold. Rollie shrugged. Made as much sense as anything else.

As the darkness closed in on him, Rollie rode into town, feeling the weight of the day grinding down on him. Seemed like he was close to heading this thing off, but there was still a lot to do. At some point he'd have to go up against Bickerstaff. That was a hard man, and it wouldn't be pretty.

Rollie's feet were dragging in the dust as he led the gray horse into the barn. Hartshorn had already gone for the night, but a bait of corn was waiting in the stall. A small smile crept onto Rollie's face. It was nice that the smith had thought about him and taken the time to set out the corn.

Rollie stripped the saddle, placing it on the fence, and hanging the blanket so it would dry. Talking softly to the horse, Rollie used a brush to wipe the gray down. He was almost finished, when he heard a step behind him. Thinking it was Hartshorn; Rollie gave the gray a pat and turned.

"Oh," he said, feeling the blood rush to his face and a small knot of fear twist his guts. "Uh, hi."

Sarah blushed, clasping her hands behind her back and turning a little away from him, then back. "Hi, yourself."

Rollie swallowed, turning the brush in his hands. "Sure is a pretty evening. Might even rain a little."

"That would be nice."

"Sure would be," Rollie agreed, seizing on the subject. "A little rain sure would green things up. Might even cool it down a mite."

"That would certainly be nice," Sarah said, shifting her feet.

Dang! Rollie wiped sweat from his brow. Sure didn't take long to talk out the weather. "Uh, did you need something?"

"No," Sarah replied, as red color flooded across her cheeks. "I just saw you ride in and thought I would come say hello."

"Thank you," Rollie said, then kicked himself. What a simple thing to say. He was still mad it himself, when it occurred to him, the stable wasn't that easy to see from the hotel. She'd been at the front window, watching for him.

With that knowledge, Rollie sucked in a deep breath and plunged in. "Say, I was fixing to go up to the café. I was thinking that maybe, you like to join me for a hunk of pie."

The smile that flowed across Sarah's face woulda made a marble statue weak in the knees. It sure sent Rollie's heart to galloping like a runaway horse.

"I would like that," she said, he voice soft as a summer's breeze.

Tossing the brush aside, Rollie took her soft, dainty hand in his rough one. Man, this was fine! As they walked, Rollie thought back to what he'd said. Wasn't exactly poetry, but dang it, it got the job done. They were gonna have some pie!

As they strolled up the street, Rollie felt his chest balloon up. He had a girl. He stole a quick look sideways at her. Wasn't a prettier gal anywhere. He was one lucky feller. He was practically strutting by the time they reached the café.

Beaming from ear to ear, he opened the door, holding it wide so Sarah could enter. Ethel Moser was washing tables, looking up as they came in. She dropped her rag, a warm smile washing across her face. "Well, look at you two," she cooed. "Are you stepping out on the town?"

"Ah…," Rollie stammered, not sure what they were doing. "Aw, we were just hunting some pie. If you had some that is."

"Got some rhubarb. Made it fresh this morning."

Rollie glanced at Sarah. He didn't really care for rhubarb. "That would be just fine," Sarah said. "I love rhubarb pie."

Rollie frowned a little. He always thought eating rhubarb was like chewing on a handful of barbed wire. "Give us a couple of pieces," he said, deciding right then and there to learn to like it.

Rollie led Sarah back to a table, pulling back a chair for her. "I'll be right back. I need to speak a quick piece with Moser."

"Okay," Sarah said, smiling up at Rollie.

Feeling like he could walk across water and not leave any tracks, Rollie hurried back to the kitchen. He found Moser cutting up a side of beef. "Hey, Rollie," Moser grunted, tossing aside his cleaver. "You still set on going out to Bickerstaff's in the morning?"

"Yeah," Rollie said, with a firm nod of his head. "I want to end all of this."

"Liable to get yourself killed," Moser observed, wiping sweat from his brow with a towel.

Rollie shook his head. "I just want to get this over with." Rollie shifted his feet, then straightened up. "That offer still there to go partners on that freighting outfit?"

"You bet," Moser said his face lighting up like a store bought lamp. "You in?"

"I am."

Moser grinned like a coon eating corn on the cob. "Say that's just jim dandy. What brought you around?"

"Aw, I don't know."

Moser leaned sideways, looking past Rollie and into the dining room. A wide grin split his face when he saw Sarah sitting at the table. "Well, I'll be," he muttered grabbing Rollie's hand. "Well, congrats, boy," he said, pumping Rollie's hand; like he was trying to bring up water.

"Thanks," Rollie said, turning back to the dining room. He smiled when he saw Sarah waiting on him. Dang, she was pretty as a bucket of butterflies.

Moser leaned back against the counter, grinning to himself as he watched Rollie wobble back to the table. That boy had it bad.

"That's nice," Ethel murmured, slipping an arm around her husband and leaning her head on his chest.

"It sure is." Moser hugged his wife, kissing her on top of her head. "Man, that boy is hooked, reeled in, and already up on the bank. All she has to do is get him in the pan and he is done."

"Shut up," Ethel said, giving him a light slap. "It's sweet."

"You bet it is," Moser agreed, licking his lips, and nodding his head several times. "That boy don't get himself kilt in the next few days, we're gonna be rich!"

CHAPTER NINE

First light caught Rollie back on the trail. He should be tired, but he wasn't. Fact was, he felt invigorated. The morning had a cool, crisp feeling. Maybe the rain was finally coming. The sky was clear but there was a feel of a storm coming. Either way, Rollie felt good.

Part of it was he felt like he finally had a grasp on things. Finally, he had an idea of what was going on and a plan of sorts to set things right. Felt good to be doing something. He even found himself mulling over Moser's offer. Rollie didn't really want to be a freighter, but it sounded like a good opportunity.

But mostly it was Sarah. Somehow, she kept crowding into his thoughts. He kept thinking of the picnic. He'd have to find just the right spot. Someplace beautiful. A place to remember.

Maybe the spot where he camped with Mort? Rollie frowned. A nice area to be sure, but it didn't fit with his image he was building in his mind. He pictured a place with a flowing stream, trees with lots of shade, and a field of wild flowers.

Rollie glanced back over his shoulder, gazing at the mountains. There would be a nice place there, trouble was it would be at least a half day's ride and Rollie would still have to find a place once they got there.

Maybe Diablo Canyon?

Naw, that wasn't quite right. Pretty enough place, but not quite what Rollie had in mind. What he needed was something special. Women now, they set store by that kinda thing.

Rollie shook his head. He'd best quit thinking about Sarah and start thinking about this morning. He wasn't sure what he was gonna do. He'd put a lot of thinking on it and, so far the best he'd come up with was to simply ride up and brace Bickerstaff.

Rollie was thinking that he could read Bickerstaff. Look in his eyes and see what the big rancher was thinking. Maybe rattle the man a little. Hopefully Rollie could shake the rancher and he would let something slip. Rollie wasn't sure he liked the plan. It certainly had one big drawback. Push a man hard enough and he's liable to push back. One thought kept tickling the back of his mind. What he was doing reminded him of the sheriff. This was exactly what the sheriff had done and that hadn't turned out so well for him. He was dead.

Truthfully, Rollie was little nervous. Bickerstaff might just up and have him killed today. Rollie was under no illusions, if Bickerstaff turned his crew loose on him. They would kill him.

Rollie didn't think that would happen. Bickerstaff might be mean and rough, but he wasn't stupid. Too many people knew Rollie was coming here. The way the mood of the country was running, a lynching was a distinct possibility. Folks have had enough.

Rollie just hoped Bickerstaff understood that.

It was just turning full light when Rollie rode into the Bickerstaff ranch. Right off, he was struck by how neat the place looked. White washed rocks had been placed to border the walkways. A dainty, white picket fence cut the house off from the rest of the buildings. Flowers had been planted along the fence and some of them were starting to bloom. The yard was freshly raked and the house looked to have a new coat of paint. Huge stones had been laid to make a massive front porch. Two rockers sat on the porch, with a small table between them.

An older woman stopped from her task of hanging laundry to shade her eyes and watch Rollie ride into the yard. "Hank, we got company," she shouted, stepping away from the laundry to meet Rollie.

"Good morning," she said pleasantly. "Would you like some coffee?"

"Never mind that," Bickerstaff barked, stepping out on the porch. "He won't be staying." Bickerstaff belted a gun belt around his waist and stepped off the porch. "What do you want?"

Rollie had decided he would take the bull by the horns and show no weakness. "I came out here to deliver a warning. You send your men in to shoot up the town again and I'll be coming for you."

For a second Bickerstaff hesitated, then sneered at Rollie. "Don't know what you're talking about."

Rollie placed his hands on the saddle horn, leaning forward a little. "I know you killed Burke. I know that was the real reason your men attacked the town."

Looking genuinely puzzled, Bickerstaff cocked his head, scratching his belly. "You're crazy. I didn't even know Burke was dead before you told me."

It was Rollie's turn to sneer. "Sure you didn't." Rollie jabbed a finger at the ranch. "I know about Diablo Canyon and Baines being out there, watching things." Rollie watched the big rancher closely, but no flicker of emotion crossed the man's face. "I know you were out there yesterday."

"Bull," Bickerstaff replied flatly. He glared at Rollie, and then laughed. "You're bluffing, cause I surely wasn't there."

"I saw the tracks," Rollie shot back, but he could feel the beginnings of doubt tickle him. Bickerstaff's attitude bothered him. If he didn't know better, Rollie would think the rancher was telling the truth. "I trailed you right to here," Rollie said, fudging the truth, trying to shake the big man.

"You're lying," Bickerstaff sneered.

They stared at each other for a long minute before Rollie wheeled his horse around. "I'll be back for you."

"I'll be here."

Rollie rode away wondering what he had accomplished here. He sure hadn't rattled Bickerstaff. Not even a little bit. But that in itself told Rollie something. Either Bickerstaff was innocent or he just didn't care what people thought. Rollie remembered the sheriff getting killed after talking to Bickerstaff. Maybe the big rancher didn't care at all. Rollie knew he'd best be careful.

As Rollie rode slowly out of the yard, Bickerstaff's wife stepped up beside him, and together they watched Rollie ride away. "Hank, what's going on? Are you in trouble with the law?"

"Naw, he was just bluffing. Just trying to spook me. He thinks I'm mixed up in all this killing and nonsense going on."

"You're not? Are you?"

"Naw." Bickerstaff dropped a heavy arm across her shoulders, giving her a rough hug. "Don't worry bout him, he's on the wrong track."

She leaned her head against him. "I don't know, Hank, he seemed awfully sure of himself."

"Did, didn't he?"

Riding slowly, watching his back trail, Rollie cut west towards Diablo Canyon. After an hour of riding he swung around. Circling wide, he doubled back.

Pulling up beside a rock foundation that seemed to push right out of the prairie floor, Rollie dug out some cornbread that Sarah had made. Munching on the sweet bread, he watched his back trail.

If Bickerstaff had sent one of his men after him, they'd be coming along soon. As he waited, Rollie kept an eye to the west. A gray line of thunder clouds was building up against the mountains. Maybe they would get the rain everyone was praying for.

As the moments trickled past, Rollie felt impatience spur him. He wanted to get back to town. There was a lot to do. And there was Sarah.

First he had to find Mort Killigan. They had to decide what to do with Rebecca, or whatever her name might be. By rights the ranch should go to Mort. Whatever he wanted to do with it from there would be up to him.

And there was Tinsworth to consider. The big banker seemed to have disappeared. So had Rebecca Moreland.

Rollie had thought Tinsworth was the one that brought in Rebecca. It was devious and underhanded. Right up Tinsworth's alley.

If so, why had Rebecca come to his room? Maybe that had been a distraction, keeping him away from the jail while they did away with Baines. Wait a minute, that didn't work. Bickerstaff was the one who ordered Baines killed. Rebecca was working for Tinsworth. Wasn't she?

Rollie cursed under his breath. He'd thought he had it all figured out, but there was something he was missing.

Rebecca now, she was a conniving woman. Maybe her coming to his room was her own idea. Rollie rolled that idea through his mind, liking it better all the time.

It made some sense. Tinsworth wanted Jim Killigan's ranch. So does Bickerstaff, but Hank knows about the gold. Bickerstaff kills Killigan. So why doesn't he move in and take the ranch? Rollie scratched the point of his chin. So why wait and give Tinsworth a chance to beat him to the ranch?

Aw shoot, that was easy to figure. Bickerstaff was waiting until Mort was out of the way. He wouldn't want that old rooster running around with that big Sharps rifle. Right then, Rollie realized why Hank hadn't killed Mort yet. Yesterday was the answer to that. Hank had been looking for the mine. He knew about the gold, but he didn't know exactly where it was. He had to wait until he knew. Plus the more he waited, the more it looked like Tinsworth was behind it all.

Bickerstaff wasn't worried about Tinsworth. When it came right down to it, Bickerstaff probably figured he could squash Tinsworth.

Tinsworth on the other hand, he's a lot sleazier. As soon as Killigan is dead, Tinsworth snuck off and recruited Rebecca. She comes in claiming to be Rebecca Moreland. Tinsworth produces a bank loan, she signs the papers, and he takes the ranch over. Of course Rebecca doesn't squawk, because she's already been paid.

But, that Rebecca is a smart young lady. She got here, took a couple of looks around and realized the ranch was worth much more than what she was getting from Tinsworth. Rollie rubbed his chin, thinking it through. She came to me, hoping I'd back Tinsworth off, he thought. Then she could squeeze some more out of Tinsworth.

Question was. Did she know about the gold?

He needed to find her.

Rollie smiled. Maybe he could get this all straightened out. With a last, long study of his back trail, he cut sideways heading towards Diablo Canyon.

He rode quickly, keeping an eye on the building storm to the west. It was going to rain, a big storm was brewing. Rollie could feel it coming in.

Rollie worried about finding Mort. If the old prospector didn't want to be found, he wouldn't be. Rollie was counting on Mort wanting to see him.

As he rode, Rollie once again noticed the curious low mound to the south. Every time he had ridden out this way, his eye was drawn to the mound. On impulse, he swung his horse around, pointing him at the mound. Letting the gray pick his pace, Rollie rode to the mound. As they rode, Rollie realized the mound was much higher than it looked from a distance.

Several hundred yards from the mound, the ground began to slope upwards. When he reached the side, Rollie saw a game trail leading up the side.

For no other reason than he had to see what was up there, Rollie started up the trail. The gray stepped slowly, picking his way between huge rocks. As he crested the top, Rollie caught his breath. It wasn't a mound at all, but some kind of crater.

Rollie whistled. It must be a thousand feet to the bottom. It looked like somebody had dug a huge round hole and stacked the dirt around the sides.

Why would anyone do that? And how long would it take? Rollie shook his head. You could put the entire town of Cordova in the bottom. Shoot, you could put Cordova and a herd of fat cows in the bottom and have plenty of room left.

Rollie turned looking away from the mound. Far to the north, he could see the faint speck that represented Cordova. Looking slightly west, he traced the green line of Diablo Canyon. Closer to the mound, the canyon shallowed. As he studied the terrain, Rollie saw a rider come into view.

The rider was moving slowly, using a small wash for cover. From ground level he would be invisible.

Rollie drummed his fingers against the saddle horn. There was no doubt it was Mort Killigan and he was heading for his claim. Mort was moving slow using every trick to stay hidden and hide his trail. He wasn't going to be happy to see Rollie.

Rollie had no interest in the gold claim, well, not much anyway. Course convincing Mort of that would be hard. Knowing he'd better get the old coot's attention before he got to his claim Rollie snatched a pistol.

He cocked it, pointing it at the sky. The harsh sound of a shot slapped across the land. For a second Rollie stared at his pistol. He hadn't fired.

Out of the corner of his eye, he saw Mort tumble from the saddle, raising a small cloud of dust as he crashed to the ground.

Rollie dropped his pistol into the holster, reaching for his rifle. He felt frantically for it, but remembered it was lying on the desk with the stock still shattered. Shoot! He needed that rifle. Never one to waste time with a lot of thinking, Rollie slapped the spurs to the gray. As the big horse jumped forward, he grabbed his pistol again, snapping off five shots in a long roll of thunder.

Rollie fired at the nest of rocks where the shots came from. He had no hope of even coming close to hitting anything. The rocks were a good mile away and even shooting from this height, the pistol lacked the power to reach the rocks.

He was hoping to scare the attacker away. The ride to the bottom of the mound was a scary blur. The gray was a big horse, but he was nimble. He went down the slope very fast, dodging the rocks and taking the switch backs like he was half mountain goat. At the bottom he jumped the last rock and bounded across the prairie floor.

As he rode, Rollie became aware that he would soon be in rifle range for the man in the rocks.

Rollie flipped the empty pistol into his holster drawing the loaded one from the other side. Not that it would do him any good. He had a lot of ground to cover before he was in any kind of pistol range.

As the gray pounded across the tough grass, Rollie bent low over the saddle. He was in trouble and he knew it.

There wasn't any way he was gonna get close enough to use the pistol. That boy up in the rocks had already showed he could shoot. He'd simply wait until Rollie got a little closer then pick him off.

Rollie's only real hope is that the shooter would simply slip away. Maybe he wouldn't want to shoot a lawman. Course, he'd already killed one sheriff, and maybe a jailer, so that was a faint hope.

As he began to pull into range, Rollie leaned even lower, gripping the pistol. How long would the shooter wait? Wouldn't be much longer.

Rollie flinched at the sound of a rifle shot, but he quickly realized the shot wasn't fired at him. He glanced sideways, seeing Mort working the action on his big Spencer rifle.

The big Spencer sounded again, then again. Rollie could see rock chips flying off the boulders as Mort shot until the rifle ran dry.

By the time Rollie reached the rocks, they were empty. He could see the shooter leaning over his horse, riding away.

Rollie pulled up, he had no intention of chasing after him. Without a rifle he would be at a disadvantage. Besides he didn't know how bad Mort was hurt. Couldn't leave the old codger lying out there.

Before turning away, Rollie studied the rider. The man was a half mile away, his back to Rollie. He was bent low over the saddle, but Rollie thought it might be Lang. There was something familiar about that blocky body. Could very well be Lang.

Turning away, Rollie trotted the gray back down to Mort. Mort was lying on his side, the rifle out in front of him. He wasn't moving and Rollie could see a smear of blood across his shirt.

Keeping an eye over his shoulder, Rollie sprang from the saddle. He didn't trust the killer to keep going. Not seeing anything, he knelt beside the old prospector.

"How you doing old timer?"

Mort coughed a little. "Feel like I been kicked by a mule, but I'm still alive."

"That's the most important thing," Rollie grunted, pulling back the old timer's shirt. Rollie took a quick intake of breath.

Mort twisted his head to look at the wound and gave a small chuckle. "Reckon you saved my bacon."

Rollie stared down at the bullet hole. He wasn't sure he'd saved the old man; the bullet hole looked to be right over the heart. He sucked in a quick, hard breath. Mort barked out a harsh chuckle. "Saw you out of the corner of my eye. I was turning when I got hit." He looked wryly at the wound. "Reckon if I hadn't turned to look,

I'd be shaking hands with St Peter and trying to explain about that one time down in Juarez."

Rollie swallowed hard, looking at the exit wound just below the left arm pit. Rollie wasn't a doctor, but he figured if Mort wasn't dead yet, the bullet didn't strike anything vital. If he didn't bleed to death, Mort would be alright.

Rollie went to his horse, pulling his bedroll off. He took out his knife cutting strips from the blanket. When he had several strips, he cut a couple a pads. Easing the strips under Mort, he placed the pads over the wounds then snuggly tied the strips securing the pads.

"It ain't much, but it should get you back into town. You think you can ride?"

"Do I got a choice?" Mort asked. "I don't know if I can get up, but you get me on the horse. I'll ride as far as I have to."

Rollie smiled down at the old man. "This is gonna hurt a bit."

"Yeah, I suppose it will," Mort grunted, extending his hand up to Rollie. "Let's get it over with."

"Ain't you the tough old bird?" Rollie said, grabbing the old timer's hand.

"You better believe it." Mort said, then swore bitterly as Rollie pulled him to his feet.

"You okay?" Rollie asked.

"Get me on the horse."

"Put your foot in and I'll boost you up."

Mort didn't waste time or energy answering. By the time he was in the saddle, his face was gray as gunpowder. "Guess I ain't as tough as I thought," he managed.

"Tough enough." Rollie said, looking sideways at him. "You hang on, I'll get you into town. Besides, you wouldn't want to die now, not with all that gold you got."

Mort held on the saddle horn, shifting in the saddle. He grinned a wicked grin at Rollie. "So you think I found gold, eh?"

"Yep. I'm sure of it," Rollie answered feeling downright smug. He waved a hand to the west. "Somewhere out by Diablo Canyon."

"You think so?" Mort shot a grin at Rollie. "Maybe, but you sure never found it yesterday, and lordy did you look."

"You saw that?"

"Sure did. And for a guy who keeps claiming that he ain't interested in gold, you shore burned some daylight hunting for it."

Rollie grinned sheepishly. "I couldn't help it. I wanted to see it."

"Well, you never found it and neither did that skunk bucket Lang."

"Lang?" Rollie asked. "That was Lang? I thought it was Bickerstaff."

"Naw, it was Lang." Mort glanced sideways at Rollie. "But Lang was riding one of Hank's favorite horses."

"Doesn't matter," Rollie decided. "I still know you found gold there."

Mort laughed, his laugh stumbling into a ragged cough. "Aw crud, that hurt," he groaned, wiping his mouth with the back of his hand. "You don't let go of a notion once you get it in your head. I tell you what; you can have all the gold I found out there."

Something about the old man's tone gathered up Rollie's attention. "No gold?" he asked, already knowing the answer.

"Nope," Mort said, cackling as Rollie swore bitterly. "Thought you had it all figured out, didn't you?"

"Yeah," Rollie replied sullenly, and then it hit him. Whatever was going on, Mort knew what it was about. Pulling his horse to a stop, Rollie stared hard at the old timer. "You better come clean with me. Somebody wants you dead."

Mort managed a shrug. "They been trying to get me and I'm still breathing."

"Yeah, for how long?" Rollie shot back. "And what if I hadn't come along today. You gotta trust me now."

Mort clamped his mouth shut, shaking his head as he looked off into the distance. Rollie swore, smacking his hand on the saddle horn. "Look, if I wanted to kill you, all I'd have to do is push you off that horse and ride off."

For a second, they sat in silence. It was so quiet Rollie could hear the faint rustle of the breeze through the grass. "I know about Rebecca and Sarah Eckles. I know that girl in town ain't Rebecca."

"Sary told you bout that?"

"Yeah, we talked some," Rollie said, then added, "We're going on a picnic."

Mort glanced quickly at Rollie. "Is that right?" he asked and Rollie nodded. "I set store by that girl. You best mind your p's and q's and treat that girl right."

Rollie nodded gravely, "Yes sir. I aim to make her happy"

"You got it bad for her, I can see it," Mort said with a dry chuckle. "I tell you one thing; you can ride a long ways and not find a better gal."

"You're right about that."

Mort started his horse, walking slowly. After a few minutes he blew out a sigh, digging in his pocket. He pulled out a rock holding it up for Rollie to see. "You know what this is?"

Rollie took it from the old man, rolling it in his fingers. The rock was surprisingly smooth and cool, reminding Rollie of glass. It had a weighty feel to it, like something valuable.

"Is it some kind of quartz?"

Mort snorted, snatching it back. "Quartz my aching backside! That there is a diamond!"

"Diamond?" Rollie repeated frowning, "I thought they were shiny."

"A lot you know," Mort said, rolling his eyes. "You got to cut 'em and polish 'em up. Do that and this baby will sparkle like a star in the sky."

"Huh?" Rollie said taking it back. It sure did feel special, solid, with some weight.

"You talk that girl into marrying you and I'll give you one to slide on her finger."

"You sure this is a diamond?" Rollie asked holding it up to the sun. It looked cloudy.

"Sure, I'm sure," Mort snapped, taking it away from Rollie. "When Jim and I went back east last year, I sold a couple. They fetched a right pretty penny too."

"Hmmmm," Rollie said, thinking it over. "So this is what this is all about?"

Mort dropped the diamond back in his pocket, turning serious, "Maybe, I don't know. I been picking the things up for a few years. I haven't found the vein where they are coming from, but I keep finding the rocks."

"You just been picking them up?"

"Yup," Mort replied smugly. "They're just scattered across the ground. Right there for anybody to find."

Rollie smiled, "So, that's why no one had found your claim. There wasn't one to find."

Mort cackled loudly. "Yup, but man it sure was fun watching them fellers hunt for it."

"You tell anybody about them?"

"Just Jim, but he wouldn't say nothing."

"Somebody found out," Rollie commented.

"I reckon. I mighta let it slip to one other person, but she wouldn't say anything."

They rode in silence, Mort hanging onto the saddle horn by sheer grit. Rollie watched the old timer out of the corner of his eye. Rollie could almost see the strength draining from the old prospector. He deserved better than this.

"I figure I'll hunt up that gal pretending to be Rebecca and send her packing. We'll get you patched up and then get you moved out to the ranch. Is there some men out there you can trust?"

"I don't know, most of Jim's old hands done moved on. That snake Tinsworth done moved in yesterday afternoon."

"Is that right?" Rollie muttered, thinking of the timing. A lot had happened yesterday. Did Tinsworth just see the raid on the town as a good chance to move or had he had a hand in it? Rollie scowled, shifting in the saddle.

Those had definitely been Bickerstaff's men on the raid. So probably Tinsworth just saw his chance and made his move. "I'll get you to town, then go move him out."

"You be careful, that's a rough crew he's got working for him."

"Yeah," Rollie said, feeling a chill. The old man wasn't just whistling in the dark. It'd take some doing to root Tinsworth out of there. Still it had to be done.

"You doing okay?" he asked, glancing over at Mort.

Mort gave a small nod, but he looked like he already had at least one foot in the grave. "Hang on old timer, it ain't your time yet."

It wasn't far, just over a mile, but it seemed like a long way. "You want to stop? I could ride ahead and get a wagon. Come back and pick you up."

"No," Mort croaked. "I just want to get there."

"Okay, hang on."

They plodded along, Rollie beside Mort holding the older man in the saddle. He could feel the blood leaking from the wounds. Mort was a dried-up, old codger and Rollie wondered how much blood the old coot could spare.

By the time they rode past the stable, Mort was breathing hard. The air was wheezing in and out of the old timers lungs like a rusty set of billows. "Hang on, we're almost there."

As they passed the barn, Rollie whistled sharply. Hartshorn rushed out of the barn, rifle in hand. When he saw Rollie holding Mort in the saddle, he dropped the rifle hurrying to help.

"How bad is he?"

"I'm not sure. He's lost a lot of blood. Didn't seem too bad at first, but he's slipping fast now."

"Let's get him over to the hotel." Hartshorn said. He got on the other side, helping to hold Mort up. "Who did this?"

"I'm not sure, but I'm going to find out."

Hartshorn shook his head sadly. "This is getting out of hand," he moaned.

"Yeah," Rollie agreed as they stopped in front of the hotel. With Mort, moaning and groaning, they got the old timer off the horse.

"Should we lay him down?" Hartshorn wondered.

Rollie grimaced as Mort groaned, his head lolling sideways. "I don't know, we got him up, maybe we should just get him inside."

They were wrestling him across the boardwalk when Sarah burst out the door of the hotel. "What happened? Is he alright?"

"He ain't good," Rollie grunted. "Who's the best doctor in town?"

"Moser?" Sarah asked, looking across at Hartshorn.

The smith nodded. "Better get him."

"Okay," Sarah said, taking charge. "Put him in the first room at the top of the stairs. It's unlocked."

"Thanks," Rollie said, as they carried Mort up the stairs. The old prospector seemed to be unconscious, but he moaned softly as they carried him up. By the time they got him in the bed, sweat was pouring off Rollie and Hartshorn's face was red as a bowl of berries.

"Man, for a scrawny-looking devil he sure is hard to handle."

Wheezing a little, Hartshorn nodded. "What happened?" he asked between breaths.

Rollie shrugged, breathing a little hard himself. "Somebody shot him. I think it was Lang."

"We have to stop this."

"I know, I'm trying," Rollie said, feeling a bit of sting from the words.

"I know," Hartshorn replied, not knowing what else to say. Both men shuffled their feet, scraping the wooden floor as they stared down at a pale Mort.

"He'll be fine, I think," Rollie said, with more hope than he felt. "He's a tough old buzzard."

"Sure and Moser, he's a pretty fine doctor. Better than you'd think."

"Oh yeah, he'll get him fixed right up," Rollie said, nodding his head. "Bet he'll be up and around in no time."

Hartshorn nodded his head frantically. "Sure. Bet you're right."

They were back to scuffing their toes on the floor when Moser burst in the room. He took one look at the pair and shook his head. "What can we do?" Rollie asked eagerly.

Moser shook his head again. "Couldn't even take off his boots," he muttered still shaking his head. He glanced up at the pair. "You two get outta here so we can get to work. If you want to do something, watch for Ethel, she's making soup, send her up."

Heads down, Rollie and Hartshorn trooped from the room. "Guess we coulda taken off his boots," Rollie admitted.

"You want to wait on Ethel I need to get back to work."

"Sure." Rollie grunted, taking a seat, feeling very tired all of a sudden. And to think, today had started so good. Even the rain hadn't come.

Rollie was closing his eyes, when he heard someone approach. Thinking it was Ethel Moser, he opened his eyes. "Mrs. Bickerstaff," he said, jumping to his feet.

"Sheriff, I need to talk to you," she said, sniffling a little.

"Okay," Rollie said slowly, he could tell she was very upset. She's going to spill the beans, he thought. "What's on your mind?"

"It's about Hank," she sniffed, obviously very upset.

"Is he involved with all of the killing?"

"No!" she said quickly. "After you left he got to thinking. You were so sure about it, that Hank went to talk to Gene Lang. Gene was gone, but the crew told him of the raid on the town. He didn't know, that was all Gene." She paused, wiping her nose. "Well that sent Hank into a rage; he left the ranch looking for Gene."

"You think he means to kill him?" Rollie asked, wondering inside if this might be Bickerstaff's way of shifting the blame all onto Lang.

"That's what he intended, I'm sure." Mrs. Bickerstaff paused, sniffling and wiping her nose with a handkerchief. "But his horse came back to the ranch this afternoon."

Rollie nodded, thinking it over. "You think he ran into trouble?"

"Gene is a hard man. I fear for Hank."

Rollie glanced at the sky. "There's a few hours of daylight, I'll tend to my horse, then go look, see if I can find Hank."

Tears running down her face, she patted his hand. "Thank you."

Rollie was rubbing down the gray, when he heard the sound of approaching horses. He could hear voices along with the hoof beats and knew something was wrong. The horses weren't running and the voices weren't screaming, but there was an urgent feel to them.

"Rollie," he heard Hartshorn hiss. "Better get out here."

Dropping the brush, Rollie squeezed by the gray horse and ran out into the street. Leading a group of farmers, Bud Swenson pulled up in front of the livery, his shirt bloody.

"What happened?" Rollie asked almost afraid to hear the answer.

"Tinsworth," Swenson said, spitting out the name. "He attacked us. Burned my barn."

"You get shot?" Rollie asked.

Swenson glanced down at his bloody shirt. "Naw, when they attacked I was running up to the house to fetch my gun and tried to jump the fence. Didn't quite make it, jammed my shoulder into the fence."

"Anybody hurt?"

"No," Swenson replied. "Just lucky though. They hit a couple of other places. Hit Johnson's place," he said, gesturing to a hulking figure behind him. "Hit them right at noon. Johnson and his boys were inside the house having lunch, and were able to drive them off."

"Lucky," Hartshorn commented.

"Yeah," Swenson said bitterly. "Tell that to my barn. And they said they would be back every day until we leave." Swenson looked squarely at Rollie. "We are here to see what you can do."

"I warned him yesterday."

"Didn't take."

CHAPTER TEN

Morning came, cool and damp, with thunderous clouds boiling in the west. Rollie had spent the night in a cold camp, a mile from Jim Killigan's ranch. He'd cut up his bedroll to make bandages for Mort, and he'd had no protection from the wind and the rain. Stiff and sore, Rollie's mood matched the weather.

Yesterday evening he had trailed Lang from the spot he shot Mort to the Killigan ranch. Rollie had kept an eye out for Bickerstaff, but hadn't seen any sign of the big rancher. It'd been dark when he reached the Killigan place, so he had pulled back and made camp.

Last night, Rollie had been tempted to try something, but he had no idea how many men were down there, or what he might be walking into.

Rollie broke camp, the weight of the job pressing down upon him. In the back of his mind lurked the thought that he might get killed here today. But mostly he was thinking that he had taken a job and so far, he hadn't done what he had been hired to do.

Rollie wasn't a fool. He didn't want to die any more than the next man. It wasn't courage that sent him out here either. While he knew there was a chance he could die this day, he really didn't think so. He could handle Tinsworth.

Figuring out a murder might not be something which came easy to Rollie, but he was right at home in any kind of fight. And right now he was mad.

Either way, come what may, Rollie was going to do his duty as he saw it. Didn't matter that the town was talking of firing him, he had taken the town's money and their trust. Now it was time to pony up and earn it.

Not that all of this made sense, because it surely didn't. How Lang and Tinsworth tied up, that was a mystery. From what Rollie knew, Lang had worked for Bickerstaff for a long time. Rebecca Moreland, or whatever her name was, she was easy to figure. Tinsworth probably had hired her to pretend to be Rebecca Moreland. Rollie smiled a little; being a shrewd woman she'd tried to up the ante.

The funny thing was, the diamonds probably meant more to all those folks than they did to Mort. Rollie would bet on that. Rollie understood Mort. It wasn't finding the diamonds that drove Mort, it was the exploring of wild country, and the looking at what was just over the next hill. Course there was always one more hill.

Rollie was like that. He'd drifted from place to place, looking for something. The funny thing was that he had come to this place with the thought of revenge in his heart, and maybe here, he had found what he had been really looking for.

The thought rushed into his mind unbidden, almost startling him. Rollie settled back into his saddle, picturing a vision of Sarah behind the counter, that beautiful smile, spreading across her face like a sunrise. He had seen nothing, no icy mountain stream or desert sunset that could compare.

Rollie shook his head, tossing away his cigarette in disgust. He best get his head on the task at hand. If he was gonna see that blonde-haired gal again, he was gonna have to dig in his heels and fight. This wasn't gonna be easy. These men had already killed to get what they wanted, they surely wouldn't hesitate to kill again. This was a time to get mean.

It never really occurred to Rollie to turn back. This was something he had to do. Once Tinsworth and Lang were locked up or dead and Rebecca Moreland dealt with, then he could start to think about Sarah.

Now, Rebecca Moreland, she worried him. He wasn't quite sure what to do with her. His plan was to bring her back to town and let the townsfolk deal with her. Providing of course she would come.

Of course she wouldn't want to come. What to do then? Rollie felt a trickle of sweat roll down his back. He sure couldn't shoot her.

Rollie had never hit a woman, and wasn't sure he could now. The last thing he wanted to do was get in some kind of a wrestling match with her. Rollie wasn't at all sure how that might end up.

A small voice kept telling him to watch her; she might just be the most dangerous of them all. Despite how she looked all pretty and soft, this was a cold, hard woman. She might kiss him, or she was just as liable to up and shoot him. Rollie grinned, best be ready for that.

Rollie was still fretting over it when he topped the rise overlooking Jim Killigan's ranch. He pulled up, looking the place over. Funny thing, with all the fussin' over this place, it was the first time he actually laid eyes on it.

It certainly was a place worth fighting for. A small, tree-lined stream skirted the back of the buildings. The trees would provide shade for the building s in the afternoon. Looking the place over, Rollie pulled his pistols, checking them over and dropping a shell in the empty chamber. Usually, Rollie carried the pistols with the hammer down on an empty chamber, but today, he had a feeling that he would need every bullet.

Assured that his guns were ready, Rollie touched a spur to the gray and headed down the slope. As he rode, he saw two figures break from the barn and scurry over to the house. Carney and Lex Taylor. Carney rapped on the door of the house, an empty sound which carried up to Rollie. Carney and Taylor turned, flanking the door as they faced him. Rollie bared his teeth in a grim smile. They had been expecting him.

Tinsworth came through the door, smoking a fat cigar, with a dejected Lang trailing behind him. They spread out across the porch which ran the length of the house.

Rollie frowned as he studied them. He would have wished they would have stayed a little more bunched, but it didn't matter. He had a job to do here.

Tinsworth might be the most dangerous, but it was Lang who worried him. Of all of them, Lang would take the most killing. Lang looked like a man who didn't care anymore. A man like that might do anything. "I reckon you all know why I'm here," Rollie said, stopping the horse in front of them. "I'm here to take you in," he added, just in case they didn't.

Tinsworth sneered, pulling the cigar from his mouth. "I don't think so. You turn that gray around and ride out of here, and you just might live to see tomorrow."

Rollie shook his head, smiling down at the big banker. "I'm going back alright, but you fellas are coming with me. Question is, will you be sitting up in your saddles or layin across them. Makes no difference to me."

"You can't really hope to kill us all," Tinsworth said, spreading his hands. "Four to one isn't likely odds. I don't think you can kill us all."

Rollie grinned a wicked smile." Maybe," he admitted pointing a finger squarely at Tinsworth's chest. "But I can sure kill you."

Tinsworth started to say something, and then stopped suddenly, as Rebecca Moreland slipped through the front door. She held herself flat against the wall sliding sideways until she was out of the line of fire. She might have been trying to look scared, but she wasn't. Her face was bright, her eyes shining brightly. She was excited by this.

Tinsworth frowned at her before shifting his gaze back to Rollie. "Be reasonable, Sheriff," he said in a cooing voice. Moving very slowly, he pulled a fat, leather wallet from his pocket. "There's over a thousand dollars in there," he said, holding it out for Rollie to see. "Take it and ride away." Having spoke his piece, Tinsworth tossed the wallet in the dust in front of Rollie's horse.

Rollie ignored the wallet, figuring it was just a ruse to get him to look away so they could gun him down. Tinsworth grinned when his trick didn't work. "Four to one, Sheriff. Be smart and take the money."

Tinsworth waited, puffing on his cigar. He expected Rollie to take the money. When he didn't Tinsworth threw his cigar away in disgust. "Take it!" he shouted, spit flying from his mouth. "There's four of us, you are going to die here!"

Rollie nodded slowly. "So are you," he said softly. "Anything happens and I will kill you right off." Rollie stared at the banker, enjoying the sight of the color draining from his face.

Tinsworth swore, but now there was a whining quality to his words.

"Take the money," Lang said softly. He'd been thinking and come to a conclusion. He spread his feet a little, digging in. "I don't want to kill you, but I will." Lang stared up at Rollie with flat dead eyes, like old marbles. "I done a lot for them diamonds and I mean to have them. If I have to I will kill you."

"I don't think so."

They all looked to see Hank Bickerstaff riding around the corner of the barn. He was riding without a saddle and was filthy and grimy, but he had the look of a hungry wolf. He rode his horse up beside Rollie. "I'm gonna kill you Gene," he said flatly, staring heavily at Lang. The two men locked eyes for a second, then Bickerstaff shook his head, and Rollie thought he imagined a touch of sadness in the big rancher. "I gave you a place and a job and you let me down."

Lang sneered, color rushing to his face. "What did you ever give me that I didn't earn twice over," Lang sneered. "I did your dirty work for years and while you got rich, what did I get? A filthy bunk in a room full of men. I wanted things. I wanted a home and a nice woman to come home to. If I have to kill you to get them, I will."

"Whoa, whoa," Tinsworth said, taking a cigar out of his vest pocket. Some of the smoothness seemed to have deserted him. Now the banker looked a bit harried. "Look, there ain't no need for this. There's plenty to go around. Do you know what Mort found? Diamonds! There's thousands of them. More than enough to go around. We can all be rich."

Tinsworth started to put the cigar back in his mouth, and then suddenly flicked it at Rollie. As the cigar flew from his fingers, a small pistol shot from his coat sleeve and into his hand.

Rollie saw the movement and the gun, as his own hand was sweeping for his pistol. He and Tinsworth fired at the same time, the crash of their shots melding into one sound. Rollie felt a tug on his shirt as Tinsworth's bullet screamed past. He saw his bullet smash into Tinsworth staggering the banker.

Everything was moving with blurring speed. Rollie was aware of Lang and Bickerstaff both firing. He saw Tinsworth drop the tiny gun and claw for the pistol belted around his waist; Taylor snatched up his own gun and fired as Rollie rolled out of the saddle. As he hit the ground Rollie lunged sideways, firing once at Taylor, slipping the hammer and firing again. The bullets smashed into Taylor, driving him back against the wall.

Spinning on his knee, Rollie snapped a shot at where Carney had been, but the gunman was gone, running headlong for the barn. Rollie heard a bullet smack into Bickerstaff with a meaty thud. He heard the rancher grunt, but stayed on his feet. Ignoring that, Rollie fired quickly at Tinsworth, the bullet catching him in the hip and spinning the big banker. Steadying himself, Rollie fired his last shot at Tinsworth, knocking the banker to the ground.

Dropping the empty gun, Rollie snatched his other pistol, but he needn't have bothered. Carney was running for the barn, but he never had a chance. Bickerstaff pulled a spare pistol from his belt and fired three quick shots. The first two bullets drove him to the ground and the last seemed to nail him to the earth.

For a second it was quiet, and despite the ringing in his ears, Rollie thought he could hear the wind whispering through the trees. He and Bickerstaff looked at each other, both of them holding a gun. "Now what?" Bickerstaff asked holding his free hand to a bloody shoulder.

"I don't know," Rollie said, with a heavy shrug. He felt old and tired. "Thought you might be dead."

"Not hardly," Bickerstaff grunted, picking at a bullet hole in his left shoulder.

"Your wife was worried. Said your horse came back without you."

"I was on a new horse, ain't got him trained. I was having trouble with the trail, so I got down was looking around on foot. Heard a mess of shooting. Spooked the horse, he took off like his tail was on fire." Bickerstaff glanced slyly at Rollie. "Mort gonna be okay"

Rollie nodded, realizing it was the shooting when Lang ambushed Mort that spooked the horse. "I think he'll be okay."

"Good." Bickerstaff nodded curtly. "You want me for anything?"

"So it was Lang who did the killing?"

Bickerstaff gave a small nod. "I guess. After you left I got to thinking bout what you said. You was pretty certain the killings were coming from me, so I trailed Lang to here."

"Thanks, I reckon you saved my bacon today."

Bickerstaff gave a small shrug, wincing a little. "Figured Lang was my responsibility. Just glad I got here in time. Had to walk over to one of my line shacks for a new horse." Bickerstaff shifted his feet, jerking his head in the direction of Rebecca Moreland, who was standing very still against the wall. "What you gonna do 'bout her?"

"I didn't do anything really wrong. I just did what he paid me to do," Rebecca said, pointing down to Tinsworth. "I didn't hurt nobody."

Rollie sighed, feeling tired as death. "You got a horse?" he asked and Rebecca nodded meekly. He bent down and picked up Tinsworth's wallet. "Take this," he said handing her the wallet, and then pointed out to the horses. "Get on your horse and go back to where you came. I ain't gonna look for you, but I see you around here again, and I will put you in jail."

"Thank you," she said, already edging off the porch, towards the barn. Rollie and Bickerstaff watched her hurry down to the barn, skirting wide around Carney's body. Bickerstaff laughed harshly. "Would you really arrest her?"

Rollie shrugged, then laughed. "I don't know. I'm not even sure I could. I think the town fired me last night."

Bickerstaff's jaw sagged a little, then he threw back his head and laughed. "You are a fool," he said, shaking his head.

"I didn't do it for the town."

Hank nodded. "That blonde-haired gal," he said, with a knowing smile. "Hang onto her. It's a good thing to have a woman beside you." He grinned a little. "Better be getting home fore mine kills me."

Hank walked slowly to his horse, swinging stiffly aboard. "Getting to old for all this nonsense."

He started to turn his horse away, but Rollie grabbed the reins. "Just so we don't have any misunderstanding. This place belongs to Mort Killigan. He can do with it what he wants."

"Whatever you say." Bickerstaff held Rollie's gaze, then a small smile cracked his lips. "We'll see if he can hang on to it."

After Bickerstaff rode away, Rollie sat on the porch, feeling like the life was about to run out of him. He needed to load the bodies and get back to town, but right now all he wanted was to sit a minute. Leaning back against the wall Rollie closed his eyes. He was thinking of Sarah when he heard a small cough.

Turning his head, Rollie saw Lang's body hump as another fit of coughing racked the gunman. Scrambling on his hands and knees, Rollie scurried to the fallen man.

"Don't bother," Lang wheezed as Rollie tore open his shirt. Lang laughed bitterly. "Reckon I'm done for."

Rollie glanced down at the four bullet holes in the man's chest and knew it was true. It was a miracle that Lang was still breathing. "Anything I can do for you?"

Lang shook his head. "Don't reckon," he said, grimacing in pain. "You sure done enough. Worst thing I ever done was bring in Baines."

"You brought in Baines?"

Lang nodded weakly. "Yeah, I needed somebody on the crew that was loyal to me and not Hank. I knew Baines from way back, thought he would be perfect, but he brought you into this. You sure ruined everything."

Rollie felt a strange sense of pleasure at Lang's words. "I just did what they paid me to do."

Lang laughed a little. "I guess you did." Lang's eyes slid closed, and Rollie thought the older man had died, but then they fluttered back open. "I shoulda never listened to her. Shoulda known all the time I couldn't trust her."

"Who?" Rollie asked as another fit of coughing rolled through Lang's body. "Who couldn't you trust?"

"That hurt," Lang grunted through clenched teeth. "I sure could use a drink of water," he croaked.

"Sure," Rollie said, hurrying to the canteen on his horse. "Who couldn't you trust? Rebecca Moreland?"

Lang didn't answer and as Rollie bent down with the canteen, he saw that Lang never would. The gunman's eyes had glazed over and his body relaxed. He was gone.

CHAPTER ELEVEN

Rollie sat in the shade just outside the hotel. It was a nice day. The rain had finally come, raining most of the night, cooling the land. Rollie breathed deep, enjoying the lingering smell of the rain. His chair leaned back against the hotel and his feet propped up on the hitching rail, he idly watched the street. He was watching the street, but he was thinking of the girl just on the other side of the door. His instinct was to go talk to her, but something held him back.

As he thought about it, Rollie knew it was cowardice that was holding him back. That surprised him. Rollie had never considered himself a coward. He'd ridden bad horses. Faced down men with guns who wanted him dead and didn't ever recall being this jumpy. Even out at the Killigan ranch, he hadn't been this scared.

But now, just the thought of going in there, made his palms sweat and his stomach heave. The thing was; the thought of not going in there made his chest ache, like a heavy weight sat on it. With a sigh, Rollie shook his head and stared down at his boots.

Trying to take his mind off Sarah, Rollie's thoughts turned to what had happened. So many had died, for just a few diamonds. Many hadn't even known about the diamonds. Lang troubled Rollie. Not that the man was dead, he'd taken his chances and lost. What troubled Rollie were Lang's last words.

What did he mean? Who was the woman he spoke of? At first Rollie thought he meant that girl, Rebecca, but that didn't really make sense either. Rebecca had been working for Tinsworth. Rollie scratched the point of his chin. Maybe she and Lang hatched up a plan to double cross Tinsworth? Course, that didn't make sense either. She wasn't even in the country when the killings started.

Rollie wished now, that he hadn't let Rebecca go. He should have held onto her for a few days and gotten some answers. If she and Lang were working together, then that would explain things and Rollie could rid himself of the nagging feeling in the back of his mind. Maybe put the whole thing behind him.

Rollie was no closer to figuring it out, and in fact was back to thinking about Sarah when Marge Ross rode around the corner of the stable. She rode slowly up the street, a beaming smile on her face and a wicker basket looped over her saddle horn.

"Good morning to you, Rollie," she chirped, her voice bright and sunny. Rollie couldn't believe this was the same woman, her face lit with a glowing smile and her hair combed. "Seems like such a lovely morning," she said, practically cooing. "Good day for sittin' although never figured you for a lazing about feller."

"Thinking," Rollie replied.

Marge glanced at the hotel and nodded. "I bet you are thinking," she said with a big grin. "And I can just guess what you was thinking about!"

Rollie had to shake his head as he climbed to his feet. Love surely did strange things. Made him all week-kneed and scared, but it had crusty Marge Ross singing like a spring bird. Course, Rollie figured it didn't hurt that she was about to marry one of the richest men in the territory. "How are you, ma'am?"

"Oh, I'm just fine and dandy. I was just bringing Mort some dinner," Marge said, her wide face actually blushing.

"Smells good."

Marge opened the basket, revealing two plates covered with napkins. One napkin was checkered the other plain white. "I made this one for Mort," Marge explained, pulling back the corner of the napkin. Rollie could see ham hocks and biscuits smothered in gravy. "He likes gravy, but I don't much care for it myself."

"Looks right nice," Rollie agreed, dancing from one foot to the other, not knowing quite what to say.

Marge replaced the napkin, dropped the lid on the basket, and looked up at Rollie. "Have you heard the news? Mort and I are getting hitched today."

The news didn't surprise Rollie, just the fact that it would happen today. Marge had spent the last two days cooing over Mort. As he thought about it, Rollie decided even though it was happening today, it wasn't all that surprising. When Rollie saw Mort earlier, Mort had been grinning like a coon. For a man who'd been shot and come mighty close to cashing in his chips, the old prospector looked awfully happy. Rollie would bet it would take a team of horses to drag the grin off the old coot's face.

A wry smile springing to his own face, Rollie wiped his hand on his pants and offered it to Marge. "Congratulations, ma'am," he said, gravely. "I know you two will be real happy together." Rollie grinned down at her. "Reckon you will be getting one of them big diamonds to slide on your finger."

Marge's face colored a flush spreading across her cheeks. "Aw, psshaw," she said, waving a hand at him. "A diamond on me would look like a silk skirt on a sow." Suddenly, Marge lurched forward sweeping Rollie up in a fierce hug. "I want to thank you, son. You sure done a bang up job setting things right. Don't know anybody who coulda done it better." She stepped back latching onto Rollie's hand with a grip that woulda done a bear trap proud. "Now, you come inside with me and talk to that girl. I know you're wanting to and I know she's waiting on you."

Rollie glanced in the window of the hotel, hoping to catch a glimpse of Sarah. "Aw, I don't know," he mumbled, hanging his head a bit. "I ain't sure she wants anything to do with me."

"Balderdash," Marge snapped, back to her old self for just a second. "Take some good advice from an old woman. Don't waste your life pinning away. You march yourself right in there and speak your mind. Take my word, she'll listen to you," Marge assured, a sly smile sneaking onto her face. "Yes, sir, she'll listen good."

"I don't know," Rollie stammered, looking at the ground.

Marge surely wasn't the type to take no for an answer, and she wasn't going to now. Hanging onto Rollie's hand, she drug him inside. Rollie didn't fight to hard, truthfully, he yearned to go in.

Marge burst through the door, towing Rollie with one hand and the picnic basket swinging from the other. "Sarah! Where are you girl?" she shouted, practically shaking the rafters.

142

Sarah peeked around the corner, a shy smile tugging at her lips. "Yes," she said, stepping around the corner and tucking a stray lock of hair behind her ear and smoothing the front of her dress. Marge gave Rollie a last tug, and branded Sarah with a stern glare. "This young man has something he wants to say to you." Marge barked, stabbing a finger at Sarah. "And if you know what's good for you, you'll listen up."

"Yes ma'am," Sarah squeaked, still smoothing the front of her dress with the edge of her hand. Her head down, she glanced at Rollie, with a shy smile that sent a warm feeling racing through Rollie's blood. "Good morning," she said, softly.

Rollie cleared his throat several times." Morning," he finally managed to croak.

"Well, then, it ain't Shakespeare, but it'll do," Marge said, clapping her hands. "I'll leave you two to your sparking. I've got some serious nursing to do."

Both Sarah and Rollie turned to watch Marge waddle down the hallway and up the stairs. As the door closed behind Marge's ample backside, Sarah turned to Rollie. "You wanted to talk to me?" she said, her voice barely more than a whisper.

"Uh yeah. Yes, I did," Rollie sputtered, as butterflies danced in his belly. What if she said no? What if she laughed in his face?

His hands feeling big and clumsy, like pie plates, Rollie mashed his hat into a ball, turning it in his hands. "I wanted to say…well, what I meant, is, I wanted to ask…."

A lump surged up in Rollie's throat and sweat ran down his back. The butterflies in his belly now felt more like fireflies. Man, this was harder than digging ditches. Unable to meet her gaze, Rollie glanced out the window at Marge's mule. Silently cursing his own cowardice, Rollie dug the toe of his boot into the wood planks of the floor, feeling stupid as that mule.

Afraid to even look at Sarah, Rollie stared hard at that mule "Well, you see, I was thinking. I was thinking that I wanted to ask you…." All of a sudden, Rollie stopped, sweat pouring down his face. His chest felt tight and he couldn't seem to get any air in his lungs.

With an effort, Rollie smoothed down his feelings and hauled a good dose of air into his lungs. You can do this, he told himself.

And he wanted to. He had never wanted to do anything worse. He looked at that mule, just do it, he told himself.

Looking out at that ugly, gray mule, Rollie's heart was beating like a trip hammer. All sorts of thoughts were racing through his mind, like sticks in a raging river. All of a sudden, one thought hit him crystal clear.

He spun away from the window, catching a glimpse of Sarah's face with hopeful smile. "Come on!" Rollie shouted, catching up her hand and almost dragging her up the stairs.

With Sarah in tow, Rollie pounded down the hallway. As they burst into the room, Rollie could see old Mort half sitting in his bed, propped up by a couple of pillows. He was smacking his lips as Marge uncovered the plate from the picnic basket.

Marge beamed at them over the plate of food. "Guess you kids couldn't wait to tell us the news," she said, passing the plate to Mort. She smiled sweetly down at the old prospector. "Rollie was gonna propose."

"Hey that's great!" Mort said, a wide grin splitting his face.

Rollie ignored Mort's words, instead watching Marge as she handed Mort the silverware. Sensing Rollie's stare, she shot a quick glance at him. She was still smiling, but Rollie could see a bright edge of hardness behind the smile and tightness around her eyes.

Letting go of Sarah's hand, Rollie sprang across the room, snatching the plate from Mort's fingers.

"Dang it, boy!" Mort bellered, struggling to sit up. "Have you gone plumb loco? That's my dinner. How's a man supposed to mend up if he can't eat his grub?"

"You eat this and you ain't never gonna get well." Rollie glanced down at the plate, and it did actually look good. "Suppose you eat it," he suggested, thrusting the plate at Marge.

"Don't be silly!" she snapped. Rollie could almost see her smoothing down her temper as she smoothed back her hair. When she continued, her voice sounded like it had been dipped in honey. "I told you, I don't much care for gravy. This is my plate," she said picking up the picnic basket.

"Boy! Have you went and lost your mind?" Mort roared still struggling to sit up.

"Ask her why she won't eat off your plate?" Rollie demanded.

"I done told you. I don't like gravy!" Marge snapped. Holding the basket close to her chest, she backed up against the wall. She barked out a nervous laugh. "Geez talk about your skittish grooms. I think this one has done went chugging around the bend."

"No," Rollie replied, dropping the plate on the nightstand. He looked down at Mort. "You eat that stuff and you won't ever see your honeymoon. You'll sure leave behind a rich widow though."

Mort shot a puzzled look up at Marge. "Baby, what's he talking about?"

Marge ignored him, her eyes locked on Rollie. "You're babbling," she hissed.

"I don't think so," Rollie said tersely. "You see, it was Joshua Burke's death that had me bothered. Who killed him?"

"Mister Bickerstaff," Sarah said quietly.

"You said so yourself," Marge snapped.

"That's what I thought, but I was wrong," Rollie admitted.

"Seems like you been wrong a lot," Marge countered.

Rollie ignored her. "See I thought it was Bickerstaff, but he never left his ranch that day."

"Says who?" Marge demanded.

"His wife."

"You believe her?" Marge sneered.

"Yeah, I do," Rollie said quietly. "So I been thinking, if it wasn't Bickerstaff, who was it? Wasn't Lang, he was right out front leading the raid. So who? Tinsworth? I don't think so. He was sitting in his office. Didn't act like a man who'd just shot somebody. Besides, I found where the killer tied his horse. He was riding a gray."

"You got a gray horse," Marge pointed out. "Comes right down to it how do we know it weren't you. What do we really know about you? And like I said, you got a gray horse."

"Yes, I do," Rollie said mildly. "But I was out in the street where everybody could see me when Burke was killed. Besides, my horse was in the livery. You can ask Hartshorn."

"You can bet I will!" Marge assured.

"Well consarn it. Who did snuff him?" Mort asked, his voice sounding hurt, like an animal in a trap.

"Somebody riding a gray horse," Rollie replied.

"Who?" Sarah asked.

"I didn't know, and that was bothering me, then I saw Marge's gray mule and it all made sense."

"Those tracks were of a mule?" Mort asked.

"No, I woulda spotted that," Rollie said glancing at Marge who looked like she had been carved from stone. "But it got me to thinking. I only saw you riding something other than that mule once, the day Burke was killed. That day you was riding a horse."

Rollie paused, getting his thoughts together. "See the other day I saw the tracks that came from the direction of Marge's place and went out to Diablo Canyon. At the time I thought it was Burke coming from town to meet Bickerstaff." Rollie grinned ruefully. It wasn't Hank who went out to Diablo Canyon, it was Lang."

"You saw him." Rollie glanced at Mort, who nodded weakly. "And it wasn't Burke he was meeting it was you." Rollie pointed at Marge, who spat on the floor.

"I thought it was Hank who shot Burke, but it wasn't. Hank's wife told me he never left the ranch that day."

"You believe her? What else is she gonna say? She's his wife," Marge barked.

"Not only that, he helped me."

"And that gets him off the hook?"

"I also found tracks that left from where Burke was killed out towards Marge's place. At the time I thought it was Bickerstaff cutting out of town after shooting Burke. I thought he circled around your place to keep out of sight, but he didn't.

Rollie nodded. "See, I never followed the tracks all the way to your place. I bet if I woulda, I woulda seen those tracks circled around and to the main road into town. It's kinda funny you showed up in town right after Ben Riggs was killed and again after Burke was killed."

"Ain't no law against coming into town."

"And I was thinking about what Lang said before he died. That he did it for her and she made a fool of him. Who her? I thought maybe that girl, Rebecca. But, no, he meant you." Rollie jabbed a finger at Marge. "He was in love with you. See I saw the note in the sheriff's book about Lang taking the cattle to your place as payment for the corn Bickerstaff's cattle ruined. I figure that is when it started. Then after the raid, he went by your place to see if Burke was dead."

Marge rocked back against the wall, fixing Rollie with a hateful glare. "You're crazy."

"Maybe, but another thing I kept coming back to was how all these folks found out about the diamonds." Rollie looked down at Mort. "You told me that you only told one person. I thought you meant Sarah, but you meant her. You were pinning after her and wanted to impress her?"

Mort didn't speak; he just groaned and sank back into the pillows finally nodding meekly.

"I kept wondering how Burke found out, but now I know she told him. I saw him out at your place when I was bringing in Baines. I don't know if he was in love with you, or just greedy. Rollie looked over at Marge who glared back in tight-lipped silence. Rollie shrugged. "Either way, once he done what you needed, you killed him."

"Well ain't you just the smart boy?" Marge growled, snatching a pistol from the picnic basket.

"Give it up, Miz Ross. You can't kill us all," Rollie said reasonably.

Marge smiled a crazy grin. "Sure I can. I got five bullets in this gun and there's only three of you."

Rollie stared at her in disbelief. The woman was dead serious. "You'll never get away with it."

Marge shrugged her heavy shoulders. "Oh, but I think that I will, but what the heck, they can only hang me once." She grinned wolfishly, waggling the pistol. "But don't you fret; I ain't got no intention of hanging. You see, I know something that you don't, mister smarty-pants. I know she's the niece."

Rollie shot a quick glance at Sarah, wondering what this was all about. White-faced, Sarah shook her head. "Don't shake your head at me, missy," Marge snapped. "I know all about your little secret. You see I was squiring around with Jim. He told me about you coming out to see him. I know he gave you the money to open the hotel."

Sarah squared her shoulders, bravely meeting Marge's cold stare. "You are right, Mister Killigan gave me the money to open the hotel, but I'm not Rebbecca Moreland. She was my roommate in school, but she died several years ago."

"Hah, I know better. I know Mort and Jim sent money to her all those years."

"I know, I kept the money, so I could stay in school."

"That's right," Mort said, weakly.

"Well ain't that touching," Marge sneered, then smiled. "This is even better. I can prove you are nothing but a scheming hussy, trying to get your grubby hands on the Killigan fortune. Course when you couldn't pull the wool over everybody's eyes and your plan fell through, you and your boyfriend here tried to murder poor Mort. Good thing I was here, or you two woulda got away with it." Marge paused, clutching her heart with her left hand. "Just a crying shame I couldn't save my betrothed."

Mort swore, a howling, hurt sound. A humiliated expression riding on his face, he sank back into the pillows. Marge smiled down at him. "Don't worry, honey. I'll make it quick. You won't feel a thing."

"Like you did with Jim?" Rollie asked stalling for time, his mind racing for a way out. It struck him funny that even though there was a good chance he might die in a few minutes, he wasn't half as nervous as when he was trying to talk to Sarah.

"Aw, Jim. There was a man. Too straight laced for his own good. We coulda had all that money and a great life together, but he wouldn't have any of it." For a second her face softened and Rollie felt a hope that they might talk her out of.

"So you had him killed?"

"No, in the end he was a sentimental fool, but I didn't kill him. It was Lang."

"He didn't really like you. He told me," Sarah said, defiantly. "He was just a lonely old man."

"He was a fool!" Marge snapped all business again.

Rollie tensed, seeing the change sweep over her face. She was going to do it! Kill them all!

Rollie had no doubts on that score. This was one hard woman. She had already killed for what she wanted. She certainly wasn't going to hesitate now.

148

Feeling desperation spur him, Rollie glanced about the room, looking for a way or at least some support. Mort collapsed into his pillows, his eyes closed, resigned to his fate. Sarah didn't look like she would be much more help. She backed up against the far wall, her hand over her mouth, as she stared horrified at Marge.

Right then and there, Rollie knew if they were gonna get out of this, it was gonna be up to him. Problem was, Marge had evidently come to the same conclusion, because she kept that big pistol aimed right at him.

For the tenth time in just a few seconds, Rollie measured the distance to that gun. The room was small, but there was at least eight feet to cover, and the corner of Mort's bed jutted out, kinda cutting him off from Marge.

Only eight feet, but it might as well be a hundred. Marge had that shooter cocked, and all she would have to do is pull the trigger. This was a cold woman. Deep inside him, Rollie knew, she wouldn't hesitate. Not in the slightest. She would fire. And from this range, she wouldn't miss.

Still he would have to try. It was in Rollie's nature. He'd go down like a hurt wolf, snapping and growling. In his mind, Rollie rehearsed what he would do. He'd dive across the room, grabbing the gun with his left hand, smashing it back against the wall. With his right hand, he'd splatter her right in the face.

Most times, Rollie didn't hold with hitting a woman, but right now, he was more than willing to make an exception. He had every intention of hitting her as hard as he could. He didn't care if he knocked her head clean off, but mainly he was just hoping to knock her out.

Rocking slightly in the balls of his feet, Rollie was ready to make his move, when suddenly; the door flew open as Ethel Moser breezed into the room. Rollie saw Marge's eyes flick to the door and he made his move.

As he dove across the room, for just a fleeting second, Rollie thought it was gonna work. Ethel's sudden appearance had distracted Marge just enough. Marge fired, and Rollie felt the searing pain as the powder burn his face, but Marge's pistol had drifted off line and the bullet sailed past is head.

A sense of triumph burst upon him. He was gonna make it. Then without warning, a bolt of pain shot through his leg and Rollie staggered. The problem was while Ethel's entrance distracted Marge, it also distracted Rollie, just a little. He forgot about the corner of the bed jutting out. Halfway to Marge, his knee smacked into the corner post. A shock of pain tore up Rollie's leg and he spun slightly sideways.

His flailing left hand slid off the gun and the punch with his right missed completely, smacking into the wall beside her head. His fist tore through the plaster, sinking in up to his elbow, as Rollie howled in pain.

The howl was cut short as he saw that Marge had the gun cocked and was trying to bring it to bear. With one hand still stuck in the wall, Rollie twisted his body, trying to keep her pinned against the wall. He grabbed her gun hand above the wrist, fighting to pin it against the wall.

The thing was Marge was a big, solid woman and mighty strong. She was desperate as well as a dirty fighter. Rollie found that out when she gouged him in the eyes and bit his arm. Blinking back the tears, Rollie staggered back, pulling free from the wall.

Cussing like a sailor on the docks, Marge stamped his foot and jerked back with her gun hand. Her arm covered in sweat was slick and it slipped out of Rollie's grasp. Marge staggered back, a quick, triumphant grin springing to her red face.

The grin melted from her face as her feet tangled into the handle of the picnic basket. Her arms flailing wildly, she crashed back into the window. For a second she hung there, and then tumbled backwards and out of sight.

Surging forward, Rollie grabbed at her foot as she went out. He got the toe of the moccasin she was wearing, but it pulled off her foot and she was gone. Rollie heard her hit with a thud, that sent a chill up his spine.

Looking out the window, Rollie saw she had landed on the back of her head and neck. Her feet were extended upwards, like she was standing on her head against the wall.

As he watched, her feet slid along the wall and she toppled sideways.

CHAPTER TWELVE

Rollie paced the Chuck Wagon Café, weaving between the tables as he sipped a cup of coffee. For the twentieth time, he looked out the window, peering down the street. Moser chuckled, clapping him on the back. "Don't worry, boy. He'll be here."

"Yeah, I know," Rollie grunted, pressing his face against the glass so he could see a few more yards down the street. "Just seems like he should already be here."

Moser shrugged crossing to the coffee pot. "It's a far piece, but don't fret, he'll get here," Moser assured, topping off his cup. "You want a refill?" he asked, holding out the pot. Rollie nodded absently, holding out his cup. Moser grinned, a twinkle in his eyes as he glanced sideways at Rollie. "Maybe you want a nip of something stronger? Something to put a little starch back in your knees?"

"You got anything?"

"You know Ethel don't allow me to keep any liquor in the café."

"Oh. Guess I didn't want anything anyway."

"Now hold on," Moser said, a sly smirk creeping onto his face. "I just said she don't allow me to keep anything. Didn't say I didn't have any."

"Huh," Rollie grunted, his mind racing too wildly to follow what Moser was saying.

"I'm saying keep your eyes peeled," Moser grunted, crossing the café to the box which held his firewood. "You watching?" he asked, as he bent down to the box.

"Yeah, yeah," Rollie grunted, feeling an irritation spur him. "No one's coming."

"Good," Moser said, dragging the box away from the wall. He shot a quick glance back at Rollie, reached into the hole in the wall and pulled out a bottle. Yanking the cork out with his teeth, Moser spit the cork across the room and took a long pull. "Had to make sure it hadn't went bad," he said, pouring a good slug in his coffee, then one in Rollie's. "You see Mort this morning?" he asked, as he replaced the bottle.

"Yeah," Rollie replied, nodding. "He seems to be doing good. Figure he'll be up and about in few days."

"Glad to hear it," Moser grunted as he slid the wood box back against the wall. "Word has it, he's gonna give you Jim's ranch?"

"I heard some talk about that," Rollie agreed, grimacing as he tasted the coffee. "Whew," he said, feeling the hair inside his nose burn.

"Yeah, that'll cure what ails you," Moser said, with a grin. "If you get the ranch, would you still be interested in partnering up on the freighting company?"

Rollie frowned, feeling a little low down. "I don't know, there's a lot of work to be done out there."

"So you're backing out on me? Gonna leave me high and dry?" Moser asked, sounding way too cheerful.

"Well, I don't know." Rollie swilled down the coffee, feeling it burn down his throat and warm his stomach. "Might not have time to do a proper job for you. I was wanting to get that mill going."

Moser bobbed his head up and down. "What I was thinking." He took a quick shot of his coffee then plunged in. "Not that we're trying to cut you out or nothing, but Hartshorn and me was talking. You get that ranch, you're gonna be a right busy man. We got another feller in mind to take you place."

"Yeah?"

"Yeah," Moser said with a crafty grin. "Course we ain't gonna offer him the deal we gave you, but he'll do okay for himself."

"You been busy."

"You betcha!" Moser said, setting his coffee aside. He paced the room rubbing his hands together. "Man I tell you boy, you sure did a bang up job. Things are rolling now. That cobbler he's coming out. He and his wife are gonna take over the store. For the first year they are gonna give half the profits to the town, since Joshua didn't have any kin. Bickerstaff bought Tinsworth's cattle. Paid the town in cash for them this morning."

"What does the town need with all that money?"

"Like I said, things are popping. We're gonna build a church and school. We're sending back east for a school teacher, gonna have to pay her." Moser shook his head like he was explaining something simple to someone who was even more simple. "See if folks are gonna move here, they are gonna have youngster with them and they'll be wanting a school." Moser was beaming as he clapped Rollie on the back. "Now that's what is gonna set us apart from all these other towns, we are gonna have a school, a good one."

"And a church too?"

"Yup," Moser said bobbing his head up and down. "We figured it out all scientific like that a town oughta have one church for every five saloons."

"What about Marge Ross' place, the town sell it, too?"

"No, dang it!" Moser said, smacking his fist in his palm. "Turns out, she had kin, a nephew of her husband's coming out to work the place."

Rollie laughed seeing that losing Marge's place really pained the big cook. "Can't win them all."

"Woulda been nice though," Moser grumped, staring out the window. "Hey, you best get ready, he's here."

Rollie's laughter melted into a red-hot panic. "He's here? Already?"

"What do you mean already?" Moser said, and then laughed. "You been staring out that window all morning. You ain't scared? Are you?"

Rollie licked his lips. "To death."

Moser laughed clapping Rollie on the back. "Don't you mean till death do you part?"

THE END